THE VANQUISHERS

BY KALYNN BAYRON

For younger readers

The Vanquishers

For older readers

Cinderella Is Dead
This Poison Heart
This Wicked Fate

THE VANQUISHERS

KALYNN BAYRON

BLOOMSBURY
CHILDREN'S BOOKS

NEW YORK LONDON OXFORD NEW DELHI SYDNEY

BLOOMSBURY CHILDREN'S BOOKS
Bloomsbury Publishing Inc., part of Bloomsbury Publishing Plc
1385 Broadway, New York, NY 10018

BLOOMSBURY, BLOOMSBURY CHILDREN'S BOOKS,
and the Diana logo are trademarks of Bloomsbury Publishing Plc

First published in the United States of America in September 2022
by Bloomsbury Children's Books
www.bloomsbury.com

Bloomsbury books may be purchased for business or promotional use.
For information on bulk purchases please contact Macmillan Corporate and
Premium Sales Department at specialmarkets@macmillan.com

Library of Congress Cataloging-in-Publication Data
Names: Bayron, Kalynn, author.
Title: The Vanquishers / by Kalynn Bayron.
Description: New York : Bloomsbury Children's Books, 2022.
Summary: In an alternate San Antonio, there have been no known cases of vampirism
since a group of masked vampire hunters called the Vanquishers wiped out the last horde
of the undead twenty years ago, but twelve-year-old Malika "Boog" Wilson's parents are
not taking any chances, especially when Boog's new classmate Aaron goes missing.
Identifiers: LCCN 2021062841 (print) | LCCN 2021062842 (e-book)
ISBN 978-1-5476-0977-2 (hardcover) • ISBN 978-1-5476-0980-2 (e-book)
Subjects: CYAC: Vampires—Fiction. | Missing children—Fiction. | Middle schools—
Fiction. | Schools—Fiction. | LCGFT: Novels. | Paranormal fiction. | Vampire fiction.
Classification: LCC PZ7.1.B386 Van 2022 (print) | LCC PZ7.1.B386 (e-book) |
DDC [Fic]—dc23
LC record available at https://lccn.loc.gov/2021062841
LC e-book record available at https://lccn.loc.gov/2021062842

Book design by Jeanette Levy
Typeset by Westchester Publishing Services
Printed and bound in the U.S.A.
2 4 6 8 10 9 7 5 3 1

To find out more about our authors and books visit
www.bloomsbury.com and sign up for our newsletters.

Remember, do not invite them in.

THE VANQUISHERS

CHAPTER 1

Vampires are extinct.

Everybody knows that. But some people just can't let the undead stay in their graves.

"It's been twenty years since the Reaping and our parents still won't buy store-brand vampire repellent. I don't get it. There's a whole aisle full of the stuff."

Cedrick is looking at me like I have two heads. I hand him the flyer I'd snatched from the mail before my mom had a chance to toss it. On one side is a picture of a plastic spray bottle filled with shimmering silver liquid and a label shaped like a garlic bulb. On the back are six or seven customer testimonials that say things like *As good as the recipe my grandmother used to make* and *I'll never use another brand as long as I live!*

"It's a Vanquisher-approved repellent," I say. "It's gotta be legit, right?"

Cedrick rolls his eyes and leans back, his elbows in the grass, his face tilted to the sky. "Who is buying this stuff anymore? Vamps are dust. They've been dust for a long time. People need to get over it." He flicks the pedal of his bike with the toe of his sneaker. "How could it be Vanquisher approved anyway? The Vanquishers don't exist anymore either."

"You know that's not true," says Jules. "They're still out there. They just don't vanquish anymore. They don't need to." They shrugged. "Even before the Reaping, vamps were almost completely extinct. And Vanquisher approved doesn't really mean anything anyway. It's just something these companies say to get people's money."

Cedrick huffs. "People out here sellin' tap water with silver glitter in it. They're lucky there aren't any vampires around for real or they could get somebody killed with that fake stuff." He sits up and looks at Jules. "You know what's actually legit, though? The repellent 'Lita makes. If a vamp got some of that stuff on them—" He whistles and shakes his head. "It'd be over."

Jules smiles wide. "Her recipe is the real deal. Store brand doesn't even have actual silver in it."

There are three kinds of people in San Antonio, people who buy their vampire repellent from the store, people who only make their own, and people who don't use any at all because they're confident the Vanquishers wiped out the last hive of the undead twenty years ago.

Most people are in that last category. They've moved on. They've let many of the old ways go. And Jules is right. Vampire populations had been shrinking for generations and there were barely any left when the Reaping happened. The San Antonio hive was the biggest one anybody alive had ever seen and it was only seven vamps strong. The Vanquishers crushed them in one epic battle that has since become the stuff of legend.

I take a bite of one of the snack bars Jules brought along. My mom's cooking tonight so I'm not supposed to be eating a bunch of junk before then but my stomach is making whale noises. I eat half the energy bar in two bites and look at the crumpled packaging, wondering if I accidentally ate some of the wrapper. It's awful.

"Is this dirt flavored?" The grit sticks in my mouth like sand. I toss the rest of it into the grass and a bird swoops down, pecks at it, then flies off. "Look. Even the birds don't want it."

"What's wrong with it?" Jules asks as they pick chunks of the snack bar out of their braces.

"Uh—it's just, you said you were gonna bring snacks and—"

"Protein bars *are* snacks. And they're healthy," Jules says. "Besides, my mom has a whole case of them in the basement and that means I can get as many as we want, for free."

Cedrick makes a retching noise. He quickly covers his mouth and looks back and forth between me and Jules. "I'll say it if Boog doesn't want to. Jules, these things taste like hot garbage juice."

"Oh c'mon!" Jules crosses their arms hard over their chest. "What did you want? Chips? Soda?"

"Yes and yes," Cedrick says. "You're off snack duty, Jules. My taste buds can't take it."

Jules rolls their eyes. "Whatever. My 'Lita says healthy snacks keep you regular."

Cedrick raises one thick, bushy eyebrow. "Regular?"

Jules grins. "They make you poop at least once a day."

I'm too old to be laughing at poop jokes but I can't help it. "I didn't need to know that." I give Jules a gentle nudge with my shoulder. "Are you mad?"

They smile a little. "Not really. I guess they do kinda taste like dirt."

We'd met up to talk about our group project that's due in a week. All the students at Victor Garcia Middle School have to make a poster for Vanquisher Appreciation Week. The anniversary of the Reaping kicks the whole thing off and it's a solid week of parties and parades. People dress up like their favorite Vanquishers—the Mask of Red Death, Carmilla, Threshold, Sailor's Knot, Argentium, Nightside, Dayside, and the Wrecking Crew. Travis Park gets lit up like Christmas and the city dyes the San Antonio River red—like blood. My mom thinks it's a morbid but necessary reminder of the past. I just think it's bad for the wildlife.

Our principal, Ms. Mason, said sixth graders could team up and make posters for the Northside Independent School

District float, which will be paraded through downtown on the final day of the festivities. I'm determined to make sure our poster stands out.

I got the poster board, Cedrick brought markers and glue, and Jules printed out pictures of wooden and silver stakes, garlic bulbs, and elaborately knotted pieces of string. I thought we could sit outside to work on it, but sweat is already beading on my forehead and I can feel the freshly greased scalp between my braids sizzling.

"We gotta put this project together but it's too freakin' hot," I say. "Let's go to my house and just get it done."

We pick up our bikes and head back across the Green, a wide stretch of grass dotted with gigantic transmission towers that separates our subdivision from a strip mall full of restaurants, nail salons, and a beauty supply store. We slip through the fence that surrounds my backyard, leave our bikes in the grass, and go up to the back door of my house. From my yard I can see Jules's grandma watching from the upstairs window of Jules's house next door. I wave at her and she waves back, then disappears. We pile into my house and stack our shoes up in the corner.

"That you, Boog?" my mom calls from somewhere upstairs.

"Yes, ma'am!"

When I'm at school, I'm Malika. When I'm in trouble I'm Malika Shanice Wilson. But most days and to most people, I'm just Boog. I don't think I've ever heard Cedrick or Jules call me by my given name.

"Wash your hands and don't eat nothing in the fridge," Mom calls back.

I look over at the fridge. I'd bet money there's something extremely tasty in there.

"Aww, Mrs. Wilson!" Cedrick hollers. "I was gonna eat everything in the fridge!"

"Not if you know what's good for you," she says. Even though we're in the kitchen and she's somewhere upstairs, I can hear the edge in her voice. She isn't playin'.

Jules laughs as they flip on the faucet and wash their hands. "I love your mom so much."

The three of us live in the Stanton Run subdivision on the northwest side of San Antonio. Our families have been neighbors on Noble Knight Road our entire lives. We all take turns at one another's houses for sleepovers and movie nights. My mom doesn't let me sleep out at anyone else's house, only Jules's or Cedrick's, and it doesn't really count because our houses are lined up right at the end of the cul-de-sac.

Jules's grandma, Lidia, or 'Lita as we all call her, makes a big dinner for everybody once a month at her house and I'm always mad that I have to eat *regular* dinner for, like, a week after. Cedrick's dads are both engineers so we always have the fastest go-karts, the best tree houses, the winningest science fair projects. My mom and dad work with Jules's mom, Celia Torres, at the University of Texas in the medical research department. We're tight. Not just neighbors and friends, we're family.

I pull Jules and Cedrick into the basement and flip on the lights. It's supposed to be my dad's rec room, with his Green Bay Packers memorabilia up on the walls but I pretty much took over. I do my homework and watch movies down here. It's where we sleep when Cedrick and Jules stay the night.

We dump all the supplies onto the table and start cutting and pasting everything to the poster board. Cedrick presses cutouts of stakes and wreaths of garlic onto the poster as Jules colors in bubble letters that read Thank you, Vanquishers!

"We should've put a picture of Sailor's Knot right up front," Cedrick says.

I shake my head. "Nah. Carmilla should be in front or at least right next to the Mask of Red Death."

"Red Death up front, all day every day," says Jules.

Cedrick smirks. "You *would* say that."

Jules shrugs. "Am I wrong, though?"

"I have another idea," I say. My mom keeps a trash can full of garlic bulbs in the basement pantry and I run in and scoop up six or seven. "Let's stick these on with the hot glue gun."

"Good idea!" Jules says.

"My dad wants to have a barbecue Friday night," I say as we pull out the glue gun and hot glue sticks. "He bought some new sandals so I know it's gonna be fire."

"Wait," Jules says, bewildered. "He never grills without the ugly ones he's been wearing forever."

I glance toward the stairs, then lower my voice to barely a

whisper. "Don't tell nobody but my mom says that his old pair were so ancient and raggedy she thinks Jesus might have actually worn them at one point."

Cedrick covers his mouth with both hands to keep from laughing but Jules cackles like a hyena until little tears roll out of the corners of their eyes.

"She put them right in the trash when my dad went on that business trip last month." I turn the poster board around and glue garlic in a neat row across the bottom edge. "When he came home he was looking everywhere for them. He finally just gave up and bought new ones."

"I'm ready," Cedrick says, rubbing his hands together. He turns to Jules. "Change of subject, but, Jules, you gotta ask your grandma to come visit our class," Cedrick says. "I don't know if you've noticed but we're not exactly any closer to our goal of being popular."

"That's *your* goal, Ced," I say. "Not mine."

"We'd be the most popular kids in school if she came up there for us," Cedrick says.

Jules shakes their head. "She won't do it. You know how she feels about all that."

Jules's grandma used to be a Vanquisher. Her code name was the Mask of Red Death and nobody knew who she was, just like all the other masked Vanquishers, until the year I was born. Somebody found out her true identity and splashed it all over the internet. She's kind of a local celebrity now. She hates the extra attention, but every time I see an image of her mask—a gleaming crimson skull—I feel proud that I know her . . . a real-life former Vanquisher.

My mom comes downstairs carrying a bucket, her plastic yellow cleaning gloves pulled up to her elbows. She's got her head wrapped in a pink scarf and she's wearing a ratty old T-shirt that has a picture of Beyoncé on the front. I don't have to ask her what she's doing. I can smell the vampire repellent before she hits the last step. She sits the bucket down under the window and I pull my shirt up over my nose.

"Mom, that stuff reeks!"

She looks at me like she's confused. "And?"

"I don't wanna throw up on our class project."

She dips a sponge in the bucket, sloshing it around, then holds it in my direction. "You're welcome to do it yourself."

"No thanks. I'm good."

"That's what I thought," she says with a little smirk. She drags the sponge over the sills of the little rectangular windows at the top of the basement wall in a clockwise motion.

I look at Jules. They mouth the word "sorry" before quickly covering their nose again. 'Lita had given my mom the home-made recipe and now we all have to suffer. It's a mixture of crushed garlic—and I'm talkin' twenty full bulbs, skins and all—and real silver pieces steeped in spring water for a month in full sunlight. The recipe comes from a time when the first Vanquishers got together in the 1800s, and 'Lita got her hands on it when she joined their ranks. She insists that we all use it to vampire-proof our houses. I should be used to the smell after all these years but it feels like every batch is more pungent than the last. I groan and try to fan the fumes away from us.

My mom glances at me. "Oh stop." She moves to the next window. "It gets the glass clean and when you use it on the sills, it keeps bugs out—among other things."

Other things.

She means vampires but she won't say it out loud right at this moment. A part of me hopes she's finally beginning to realize how silly it is, or maybe she's tired of keeping up her defenses when she knows there's nothing to worry about anymore.

"That smell keeps people out, too," I say. "It smells like musty armpits in here, Mom."

"It smells like cleanliness and safety," she says as she moves on to the last window. "You kids like to be funky and reckless. Not in my house."

"I smell like roses," I say. "And rules are meant to be broken sometimes, Mom."

Mom smiles, but it's the smile she flashes when she has just heard something that makes zero sense. She smiles at my dad like that a lot. "Which one of your little friends told you that?" She chuckles. "Oh, they lied to you, baby."

She finishes up her vamp-proofing that she swears isn't really vamp-proofing, then takes her bucket back upstairs.

"Y'all wanna ride with me?" my mom calls down a few minutes later. "I need to take some supplies to Tasha and Eric downtown. They're running a booth this year for Vanquisher Appreciation Week."

"What kind of booth?" Cedrick asks. "A turkey leg booth?"

"Uh, no," my mom says.

Cedrick looks extremely disappointed. "So no food?"

My mom chuckles from the top of the stairs. "No, but you're staying for dinner, aren't you? I got some baked mac-n-cheese with your name on it."

Cedric is already out of his chair and heading up the stairs. "You ain't got to tell me twice. All I heard was mac-n-cheese. You don't have to say anything else."

Me and Jules look at each other and shake our heads before we follow him upstairs.

Downtown San Antonio is decorated for the week-long festivities celebrating the Vanquishers' final victory over the undead. Giant light-up stakes hang from lampposts and the trucks hauling red dye for the river are parked along the streets. Murals showing the Vanquishers as they appeared on the day of the Reaping—battle weary, roughed up, but determined to save the city from the last horde of bloodsuckers—have gone up on the St. Mary's Strip alongside paintings of Selena and the San Antonio Spurs. The Vanquishers are as much a part of

San Antonio as anything else. Even the Tower of the Americas will turn all its interior lights red to celebrate.

We stop a few blocks over from Travis Park and help my mom haul out several bags of fake wooden stakes for her coworkers, Tasha and Eric. Jules falls in step with me as Cedrick bobs along next to my mom, talking her ear off.

"It's a perfect replica of Carmilla's crossbow," Cedrick says. "I got the proportions down perfectly. It's legit."

"When you say legit do you mean not legit at all because your bow is made of wood and duct tape?" I ask.

"Well, I can't make it out of real silver, Boog," Cedrick says, rolling his eyes. "I had to improvise."

"I'm sure it's great, baby," my mom says.

Travis Park is set up for all the festivities. Booths selling Vanquisher T-shirts and replica weapons line all four sides of the park, which takes up an entire city block. At the center of the greenspace is an octagonal platform topped with a silver dish holding a flame that is never extinguished. It's a monument to Dayside—one of the Vanquishers who died during the Reaping. Inscribed wooden stakes and silver trinkets litter the ground around the memorial. People leave them as tribute to Dayside even all these years later.

A wooden platform has been erected on Navarro Street and performers are rehearsing some weird routine while dressed as Vanquishers. The person in front has a pretty good replica of Threshold's signature tactical vest and one of the other performers is swinging a silver rope over her head but they're all dancing and lip-synching to Selena's "Baila Esta Cumbia."

"Wooooow," Jules says. "Tell me you're from Texas without actually telling me you're from Texas. Vanquishers, Selena— all they're missing is a backdrop of the Alamo."

"This is a good song, though. And Dollar Store Threshold is killin' it," I say as we spot Tasha's booth on the opposite side of the square.

We deliver the fake stakes to Tasha, who lets me, Jules, and Cedrick test out the games she's invented for the festival. The stakes are plastic and their centers are hollow. Darts are glued inside and we take turns throwing them at life-sized cardboard cutouts of vampires.

"Whoever made these targets did a really good job," I say, slinging a dart and hitting the paper vamp in the right eye.

"Eric understood the assignment." Tasha laughs. "He grabbed some photos from the archives—made it as realistic as possible."

The vamp's jaw is slung open wider than a human's and eye-teeth that look like a snake's curved fangs poke out from under its top lip. The eyes are painted black with red slits in the center. Looking at it sends a little chill up my back. I can't imagine what it must have been like to see a vampire in the flesh.

Cedrick throws a dart and hits the vampire cutout in the hand.

"Ummm, I really need to work on my aim," Cedrick says.

"Don't worry, sugar," Tasha says. "You'll never have to worry about doing it for real, thanks to the Vanquishers."

My mom smiles but she's so bad at being fake it's almost painful. Her eyes are narrow and she clenches and unclenches her jaw as Tasha goes on and on about the Vanquishers. Her favorite one is Sailor's Knot. I know this because she brings it up every time I see her. She also claims to have a piece of one of his fabled silver-infused ropes but I've never actually seen it.

"Let's roll," my mom says. She gives Tasha a hug and we head back to the car.

Back at the house, I look at our poster. I'm a little concerned it's not as flashy as it needs to be.

"What do we think?" I ask. "More glitter? More garlic?"

Jules sprinkles some red glitter on a line of glue at the top and holds the whole thing up. One of the garlic bulbs falls off and rolls across the floor. Me and Cedrick step back to get a good look at it. I snap a picture with my phone.

"Trash," says Cedrick.

"It is not," I say, picking up the rogue garlic bulb. "It's gonna stand out."

"How many points do you think we're gonna get?" Jules asks.

Cedrick claps his hands together. "Negative fifty points."

Jules shoots him a dagger of a glance. "You got a better idea?"

He shrugs. "Put it in the trash?"

"Okay. Okay," I say before they can start arguing. "I think it looks good and there isn't room for anything else. It's done. Let's watch a movie."

We put all our craft supplies away and Jules sits with me on the couch. Cedrick turns on the TV and we ro-sham-bo to decide what movie it's gonna be. I win, and I pick *Black Panther* even though we've seen it twenty times. Mom calls us up for dinner around six.

"Let's show my mom our poster," I say.

Cedrick shakes his head. "Do we have to? I think we should show it to the least amount of people possible."

I grab the poster and we scramble up the stairs. As Jules and Cedrick wash up, I present my mom with our project.

"What do you think?" I ask her.

She tilts her head to the side and looks it over. "How'd you get the garlic to stick on there?"

"Hot glue."

"Did y'all clean up?"

"Yes, ma'am. But come on, Mom, tell me what you think of our project. It's gonna be on the float downtown."

Her eyebrows push together. "Is it?"

The sound of a key in the front door draws my attention away from the fact that my mom is avoiding my question, and my dad comes in with his workbag slung over his shoulder. He sits on the little bench in the entryway and takes off his shoes.

"Hey, family," he calls. He comes into the kitchen and gives my mom a kiss.

"Did you have a chance to stop by the store?" Mom asks.

Dad pretends to be confused but I can see he's got a plastic bag behind his back.

"Tre. Do not play with me," Mom says. "I need to season that chicken tonight."

He laughs and hands her the bag. "That's why I'm running a little late. I was on the south side and decided to just stop at the store over there."

Mom glances at her watch. "It's, like, six o'clock."

Dad shakes his head. "I always forget that they still do daylight hours only over there. I went to three different stores before I realized what time it was."

The grocery stores on the south side of San Antonio close at 4:00 p.m. on the dot. Stores that work like that call them "daylight hours." They open and close while the sun is still up—no exceptions. It's another little remnant of the past when everybody was supposed to be inside way before the sun went down. Most places don't do that anymore but some stores just decided to roll with it.

My dad gives me a hug. "How's the project coming? You have everything you need?"

"We're done. It looks good. See?" I hold up the poster and he smiles.

"She's lying, Mr. Wilson," Cedrick says from the doorway.

"What do you think?" I ask him.

"Y'all are creative," my dad says. "Just—just so creative." He turns to my mom.

"Oh, so nobody is gonna say they like it?" I ask, looking at the poster again. Is it trash? I didn't think so before but now I don't know.

"It's fine, baby," Mom says.

"Should have put a picture of Carmilla on there, though," Dad says.

Mom tilts her head to the side and mean mugs my dad.

He shrugs. "C'mon now, babe. You know Carmilla's my fave."

Mom rolls her eyes. "Then why don't you go ask Carmilla to make dinner."

Dad sweeps her into a hug. "Don't be mad. She ain't got nothin' on you, babe."

Mom tries to scowl at him but she can't keep a straight face. She bursts out laughing, then shoos him away. "Put your poster up, Boog. You're getting glitter everywhere."

I set the poster on the counter and wash up.

My dad gives my mom another kiss. "Need any help in here?"

"Nah, I'm good," Mom says. "You're on dinner duty tomorrow."

"Yes, ma'am," my dad says as he nudges me out of the kitchen. His little half smile tells me we're gonna get pizza

17

tomorrow night and I'm already planning what toppings I want.

"My dads make dinner together almost every night and it's annoying," says Cedrick.

My dad laughs. "They get down in that kitchen, Ced. You can't deny that."

"They *think* they can," Cedrick says as he eyes the dish of mac-n-cheese my mom sits on the table. "But I don't wanna eat mushrooms every day."

"They back on their vegan kick?" Mom asks as she sets another serving dish on the table.

Cedrick nods like it's the worst thing that's ever happened to him. I pat him on the shoulder. "It can't be that bad."

He looks me dead in the face, his brows pushing together. "You ever bit into something thinking it was gonna be chicken and it turns out to be cauliflower? It's not right and I hate it."

I have to bite the inside of my cheek to keep from laughing. He looks so sad, but Mom always feeds us like we aren't going to eat for days and at the end of the meal Cedrick can hardly breathe he's stuffed himself so full.

Jules leans back in their chair. "That was so good, Mrs. Wilson."

"Thank you, baby," Mom says, smiling. She glances out the dining room window and her face changes just slightly. Nobody else is paying attention but I see it. Her jaw is set, she sighs. The sun is setting, turning the sky outside bright orange.

"I can help with the dishes," Jules says.

"While I have Boog right here?" Mom asks, shaking herself out of her thoughts. "She can load the dishwasher."

Jules huffs. "'Lita says the dishwasher is for decoration."

My mom laughs and pats the back of Jules's hand. "Don't feel bad, Jules baby, my mama was the same way. She didn't *believe* in dishwashers. We had one in our house the whole time I was growing up and we only ever used it as a drying rack."

I only have to do the dishes by hand when I'm washing the fancy plates during the holidays and neither of my parents ever let me forget how they didn't have that option when they were kids.

My mom pushes away from the table and stands up. "Let's get you all home."

I walk Jules and Cedrick to the porch, where my dad rests his hand on my shoulder. The streetlights flicker on down the street. I'm not allowed off the porch after the streetlights come on.

Ever.

"See you tomorrow, Boog," Jules says. "Don't forget the poster." They give me a big hug.

"I won't. I promise."

Cedrick waves and my mom ushers him down the driveway and out onto the sidewalk. They bob along behind the hedges and pop up in Cedrick's driveway directly next door to the right, and his dad Mr. Ethan is waiting for him on the porch. He waves at my mom.

"Thanks, Samantha!" he says as Cedrick goes inside.

"No problem," my mom calls back. "Tell Alex I said hi." She turns and takes Jules to their house, which is directly on our left. 'Lita meets them at the door and she and my mom talk for a little bit before Jules gives me a wave and goes inside. My mom walks back to our house, glancing down the street before hurrying up the drive.

"Let's go, Boog," she says. She loops her arm under mine and pulls me toward the door.

My dad glances over his shoulder, down the street. He's got the same faraway look on his face that my mom had at dinner.

They tell me there's no reason to be afraid of the dark, that there are no monsters waiting for me in the shadows. But even still, I'm not allowed out after dark for any reason—not to run and grab something from the car, not to make sure my bike is locked up, not for anything. Vampires have been extinct for as long as I've been alive, but the monsters still live in the memory of people like my parents—people who grew up in a time when precautions were taken on the off chance that they'd come face-to-face with one of the terrifying creatures. I can't blame them for looking over their shoulders a little more than most people but there's nothing to be afraid of anymore, and we have the Vanquishers to thank for that.

CHAPTER 2

A few minutes before the bell rings, I take my seat in the front of Mrs. Lambert's homeroom class. Jules slides into the seat next to me and Cedrick sits right behind us. I pull a bright yellow folder stuffed with loose papers and worksheets out of my backpack. On the front is a mural of the Vanquishers, with their names in small print underneath—the Mask of Red Death, Carmilla, Threshold, Sailor's Knot, Argentium, Nightside, Dayside, and the Wrecking Crew. I've traced over Carmilla's crossbow so many times it doesn't even look like a weapon anymore. On the inside flaps are a list of vampire repellents and a few of the vampire rhymes everybody learns in preschool. I read one of them to myself.

> *Bulbs of garlic, holly branches*
> *Silver shavings, sunlight dances*

Don't invite them through the door
Keep me safe forevermore

They say vampires were confused by rhymes and that reciting one, no matter how simple, could distract them long enough to make a quick getaway. I just want to know what kind of undead monster could drain me of all my blood and turn into a swarm of bats and shadow but couldn't handle hearing nursery rhymes. Something never sat right with me about that.

I find my reading log and set it aside before pulling our carefully rolled poster from my backpack. Glitter and garlic skins litter the inside of my bag. I gently unroll it and set it on my desk.

"Is there, like, a prize for best poster?" Jules asks, beaming. "Because we deserve a prize."

"I hope we get a good grade," says Cedrick. "My dad keeps saying it's harder to bring a bad grade up than it is to just keep good grades and I'm not tryna be rude, but I think he's lying to me."

"We're gonna get a good grade," I say. "Don't worry. It looks great." I'm just going to keep telling myself that.

I look around our first period classroom. Nobody else has even brought their posters in yet. I smile to myself. We're ahead of the game. Cedrick pulls at the back of his neck and huffs loudly.

"What's wrong?" I ask.

"My dad tried to edge me up. You'd think somebody who designs robots could work a pair of clippers. I think he shaved off the back of my skull."

I twist around in my seat. "Let me see."

Cedrick turns around. A big red scratch runs across the back of his neck.

"Dang," says Jules. "What did he use—an ax?"

Cedrick turns back around. "That's what it felt like. A rusty one. Now I'm probably gonna get—what's that called when you get cut by something rusty?—rabies?"

"Nope," Jules says. "Tetanus."

"Right!" Cedrick says, touching the back of his neck. "I'm gonna get tetanus."

"It's not too bad," I lie. "But listen, are we doing a *Stranger Things* marathon this weekend after the BBQ? Whose house are we staying at?"

"It's been a minute since y'all came to my place," says Cedrick.

My dad was right about Cedrick's parents, they can cook, and the more I think about his stepdad's famous blueberry pancakes, the more staying at his house seems like a good idea.

"I'm good with that," I say. "So we just link up after the BBQ?"

We all nod.

I hand our poster to Jules just as Mrs. Lambert comes into the classroom, a coffee cup in one hand, a bag full of books and papers slung over her shoulder. She's wearing jeans and a gray T-shirt, her hair cut in a sharp bob just above her shoulder.

"Well, well, well," she says, eyeing me. "The Squad got a jump on their project." I smile wide and she comes over and pats my shoulder. "Great job." She takes our poster and puts it on her desk, beaming.

Someone huffs loudly from the back of the class and while everybody else turns to look, I don't have to. I already know who it is.

"They got a jump on it because their parents never let them out the house," Adrianna grumbles.

I want to sink down in my seat and disappear. Adrianna can't stand me. I've never done anything to her, but she hates me just the same. I ignore her most of the time but sometimes she pushes things too far. Ever since she found out that me, Cedrick, and Jules have families that are a little stuck in their old ways when it comes to vampire-proofing our lives, she's made it her job to rub it in our faces. Adrianna didn't have to stay in after dark or even use vampire repellent on a regular basis. She thinks it's all ridiculous, and the worst part is—she's not wrong. I just wish she wasn't so loud about it.

"Malika can't even check the mail alone," Adrianna says. "Her mommy's too scared a big bad vamp is gonna jump out and get her."

I turn to glare at her and she grins wide. Her blond hair is pulled back in a ponytail so tight it's making her five-head look like a piece of glass. She clicks her tongue between her teeth, and her sidekicks, Emma and Leighton, giggle and roll their eyes.

"Would you like detention today or tomorrow, Adrianna?" Mrs. Lambert asks.

Adrianna whips her head around. "Detention? For what?"

Mrs. Lambert turns her back and writes the date on the whiteboard along with Adrianna's, Leighton's, and Emma's names. "For bullying. Keep it up and it'll be in-school suspension."

Mrs. Lambert angles her head so I can see her face. She winks at me, which sends Adrianna into a silent rage. Jules and Cedrick are doing everything they can to keep from laughing. This is why Mrs. Lambert is my favorite teacher. She's stingy with homework and lets us retake tests and quizzes as many times as we need to. She calls me and my friends the Squad because we do everything together. I think she knows that our families seem to be the last ones in the school still hanging on to the old way of doing things and she feels bad.

"All right, class," says Mrs. Lambert, moving on. "Take out your planners and let's get organized for the week. Remember, if you need help, you have to ask because I can't read minds."

A fly buzzes near my ear and I swat it away. It lands on my desk and struts around on my papers like it belongs there. "Mrs. Lambert," I say. "We gotta do something about these flies." I flick the fly and it buzzes off.

Ever since spring break our classroom has been swarmed by all kinds of gnats and flies. They're everywhere. Mrs. Lambert has a dozen sticky traps dangling from the ceiling and enough plastic fly swatters for everyone in class to have one.

"I've let the front office know," she says, setting a piece of paper over the mouth of her coffee cup so one of them doesn't find its way into her drink. "They need to hurry up and figure it out. Flies are disgusting and unsanitary." She's got a faraway look in her eyes, like dealing with the fly infestation on top of her regular teaching duties was just too much to ask.

The classroom door bounces open and our principal, Ms. Mason, comes in. She reminds me of my grandma. She's nice but her wig is always sitting back a little too far on her head and she always looks like she's sweating. A tall, older man in an ugly green sweater, his head so bald and shiny the classroom lights bounce off it, trails behind her.

"I'm sorry to interrupt, Mrs. Lambert," says Ms. Mason as she shuffles into the room in her kitten heels and maroon skirt suit. "I'm giving our new guidance counselor, Mr. Rupert, a tour and I wanted to stop in and have him say hello."

"Whose granddaddy is this?" Cedrick whispers.

I look down into my lap to keep from laughing.

"Just wanted to show my face," Mr. Rupert says, smiling stiffly.

I look up as his gaze sweeps over the class and stops on me.

He narrows his eyes suspiciously and I glance at Jules, who just shrugs.

"If you need anything, you know where to find me," he says. I think I hear him mumble something under his breath as he turns and walks out.

Ms. Mason exchanges confused looks with Mrs. Lambert.

"Did he mention which room he'll be in?" Mrs. Lambert asks. She and Ms. Mason share a quick laugh and shake their heads.

"He's in office twenty-seven," Ms. Mason says. "Have a good day, students. And remember to make your posters really stand out. We want to have the best float in the city for Vanquisher Appreciation Week." She turns and leaves and Mrs. Lambert sits down at her desk.

"Mrs. Lambert?" Cedrick asks. "Whose pawpaw was that and why was he wearing a sweater when it's, like, ninety degrees outside?"

Mrs. Lambert takes a sip of her coffee, smiling. Everyone laughs and we get on with our morning meeting and planning for Vanquisher Appreciation Week.

I watch the clock, impatiently waiting for class to be over because I have gym next period, with Adrianna, and we're supposed to be doing dodgeball. I picture myself *accidentally* beaning her with one of the red rubber balls.

As soon as the bell rings, I shove my folders in my backpack, wave to Jules and Cedrick, and head out the door. I run right into Mr. Rupert and he stumbles back, catching himself on the wall.

"Sorry!"

Jules and Cedrick rush over to see what happened. Mr. Rupert rights himself and scowls at me.

"You didn't see me?" he asks, an edge of annoyance in his voice.

"Uh, no," I say. "Sorry."

"Eyes up, Miss Wilson," he says.

I'm confused. I bumped into him but he's acting like I drop-kicked him across the hall.

Mrs. Lambert comes up behind me and rests her hand on my shoulder. "Everything okay out here, Malika?"

"Yeah, um, we're good. I think." I brush past Mr. Rupert and head down the hall with Cedrick and Jules at my heels.

"What's his problem?" Jules asks. "And why does he already know your last name?"

I shrug. "No idea but he's got anger management issues."

"I gotta go all the way to B building," Cedrick says. "Meet you guys at lunch?"

"Yup," Jules says.

He hurries off and I wave bye to Jules. As I turn toward the gym I catch a glimpse of Mr. Rupert at the other end of the hall—he's staring straight at me, the same expression of slight annoyance and suspicion stretched across his angular face. I turn my back and speed-walk to the gym.

In PE, I dress out and pull my braids up on top of my head, securing them with an oversized hair tie. I jog onto the basketball court to walk-run laps, enough to get credit but not enough to get too sweaty.

"Keep going, Wilson!" Coach Acosta calls after me. All eyes on me today, I guess.

We finish our laps and pair off to do crunches and push-ups. I get stuck with Larenze, who always makes everything a competition even though nobody asked him to.

"Come on, Boog," he says as he holds my feet. "You gotta do at least fifty."

I lie back on the plastic mat that feels like it's stuffed with concrete. "I've done four and don't feel any new ab muscles so really, what's the point?"

Larenze laughs as he lifts his arm to flex his nonexistent bicep. "We gotta stay in vampire-hunting shape."

I sit up and stare at him. My dad makes similar comments about staying in vamp-slaying shape whenever I complain about PE. "Not you too."

Larenze's mouth turns down at the corners. "I'm joking, Boog. Nobody really thinks we need to be prepared like that anymore. Just weirdos who don't know how to let all the vampire stuff go."

I sigh and look away.

"Hey. Sorry," Larenze says quietly. "I'm not tryna make you feel bad. I know your parents are—"

"Vampires are extinct," I say, cutting him off before he has a chance to pity me too much. "The Vanquishers wiped them out. Nobody has seen a vampire since the Reaping and even back then, most of them were dead. I know all that stuff. Just because my parents are old school doesn't mean I don't know that."

Larenze shrugs and shoots me a tight smile. "I heard somebody out in Converse was acting weird at his job so they put him in quarantine. They found two holes in his neck."

"Who is *they*?" I'm irritated now. This kind of gossip is exactly why my parents never quite let go of all their little vamp-proofing habits and I hate that Larenze is helping spread it around. "What does acting weird even mean? And *who* exactly put him in quarantine? What's this person's name?"

Larenze throws his hands up. "I don't know. I didn't ask all that. It's just what I heard."

There is always some rumor about somebody being bitten, somebody who didn't show up in a picture, or who couldn't come into somebody's house without an invite. None of that does anything to calm my parents' anxiety.

"Maybe stop spreading rumors," I say. "Especially when you don't have any facts."

"If I had facts it wouldn't be a rumor, would it?" Larenze asks.

I scoot away from him and finish my sit-ups just as Coach announces that we're skipping dodgeball to pick up litter on the softball field. I glance at Adrianna, who scowls at me. We might not be playing dodgeball but on the plus side, Coach Acosta says we're learning the electric slide next week, and I know I'm gonna get the opportunity to aggressively dance across Adrianna's toes.

When the bell rings, I change back into my school clothes, reapply my deodorant, and head to the cafeteria. I grab a tray and as soon as I get my pizza and sit down, Jules falls into the seat next to me.

"Guess what kind of homework I have?" they ask. "Algebra. I hate it. Letters don't belong in the same equation as numbers."

Cedrick joins us and starts picking the pepperoni off his square-shaped pizza slices.

"I saw Mr. Rupert again in the hall when I was going to PE," I say. "He was staring into my eyes like he was tryna read my mind."

Cedrick takes a bite. "He poked his head in my class in B building. Said he was saying hi—again. I felt like he was looking right at me." He claps his hands together as his thick eyebrows shoot up. "Does he wanna fight me? Cuz I'll knock a old man out, no problem."

Jules rolls their eyes. "Ced, you have the softest baby hands I've ever seen. You aren't knockin' anybody out."

Cedrick looks down at his hands, then shakes his head. "Why is he so worried about us, anyway? He needs to mind his business."

I nod. "He needs to keep an eye on that one boy—what's his name—Jimothy?"

"Jimothy?" Cedrick asks, milk dripping out of the side of his grin. "Please tell me that's not his real name."

"His name is Jim Allen or Jim John, somethin' like that," Jules says. "And yeah. I told Ms. Mason about him because he was askin' way too many weird questions in chemistry. He wanted to know if blood will clot when it's outside your body. Who asks that?"

I scrunch up my nose and pick at the end of one of my braids. "Yeah, see. He's a serial killer for sure."

"That's who Mr. Rupert needs to be watching," Jules says. They pull out a plastic container filled with homemade food. It smells so good it makes me want to throw my pizza in the trash. They spoon a scoop of rice and pigeon peas and fried plantain onto my plate.

"Did 'Lita give you that sauce to go with it?"

Jules fishes around inside their lunch bag and pulls out a little container with plastic wrap stretched across the top.

"I can't believe it's just mayo and ketchup," Cedrick says. "Why is it so freakin' tasty?"

"Mayoketchup is better than mayo or ketchup alone," says Jules. "That's just the facts."

"So back to Mr. Rupert," Cedrick says. "He's a creep and he's nosy. We don't even go to the guidance counselor like that so we shouldn't have to see him around too much."

"True," I say. "So, BBQ at my house on Friday. Don't forget."

"I can't wait," says Cedrick. "My dad is bringing banana pudding."

My mouth immediately starts watering. "Friday needs to hurry up and get here."

At the end of every school day, me, Ced, and Jules meet up by the bike rack so we can ride home together. The sun has made my chain the temperature of lava and I fumble with the bike lock, trying not to burn myself.

Jules walks up, shaking their head and looking at a piece of paper like they can't make sense of what's printed on it. "I have to get started on this homework. I'm so bad at math."

"I can help," I say. "Let's just go to my house. I bet there's leftovers from last night."

Cedrick meets us at the bike rack and we pedal around the side of the school and through the field out back, following a narrow path worn down by all the kids who take the shortcut to get back into the neighborhood. I spot someone standing by the gate. As we ride by, Cedrick and Jules laughing as they pretend to swerve into each other, I recognize who it is.

Mr. Rupert.

I put my head down and go by him as fast as I can, avoiding his gaze. For the one quick moment I look up, I meet his eyes, and he looks angry.

I leave him behind and focus on the only thing that really matters right now—the BBQ. We cook out on a regular basis during the spring and summer but this BBQ is special. We're kicking off Vanquishers Appreciation Week in our own way. The party downtown is always a blast but it's lots of people with fake Vanquisher weapons and masks. It can get a little sketchy so we almost always plan a big BBQ at the house for just us. We'll play music and maybe convince my dad to break out some of his old dance moves, which he swears we don't know nothin' about. And the food? My mouth waters just thinking about it.

At my house, we leave our bikes in the driveway and pile inside.

"Shoes off and wash up," my mom calls before she even sees us.

Jules and Cedrick go to the sink as I step into my mom's office. It used to be a sunroom, but my parents and Jules's mom spent the summer converting it so that she could have her own space. The back wall is made entirely of glass. It's hot as an oven and my mom's got a fan going that's pushing around all her papers.

"Mom, can I talk to you?"

She glances up and I walk over to her desk. It's strewn with half-filled notebooks and colorful folders. The wide shelves against the wall are jam-packed, mostly with textbooks and titles that have to do with her job: anatomy, physical therapy, wound healing.

"What's going on?" my mom asks.

"Uh, so, we have this new counselor at school, Mr. Rupert, and uh, he's—" I pause.

My mom tilts her head. "What is it, Boog?"

"He's kind of a creep."

My mom crosses her arms and stares at me. "I'm going to need you to give me a little more information than that."

I tell her what happened, how I felt like he'd been watching me and Cedrick and how he'd known my last name before he had any real reason to. I also told her he was mean muggin' me as I rode home from school. Even as I say it, it sounds dumb.

Mom massaged her temple. "Boog, baby, it's his job to know all the kids at school." She shuffles some papers around in front of her. "I wouldn't worry too much but if you want I can shoot your homeroom teacher an email. What's her name again?"

"Mrs. Lambert," I say.

"Right," she says. "I missed her at the open house so I probably need to reach out and say hello anyways."

"I mean, school's already halfway over," I say.

Mom blinks and then purses her lips. She's so smart. She's the person I look up to the most and I love her more than anything but she gets so focused on big things that sometimes the little stuff, like knowing my homeroom teacher's name, falls through the cracks. I try not to let it bother me too much.

"I've been so busy at work," she says quietly. "We've made some huge progress on our wound-healing serum. It can heal an open, oozing gash or abrasion in less than a day and—"

"Mom! That's gross!"

Mom is a research associate at the University of Texas. She's a doctor and she works in a lab where she studies how vampires were able to heal from injuries that would have been deadly to humans. Her department is hoping they can use their knowledge to help regular people heal up quicker. They have samples of vampire flesh and bone and one time I even heard her say they had an intact, but headless, vampire corpse. I'm not supposed to know that, though. Her eyes light up when she's talking about her research but sometimes it's too gory to stomach.

"Sorry, Boog," she says quickly. "Listen. I've been busy but that's not an excuse." Mom clicks around on her keyboard. "I'll email Mrs. Lambert right now."

"No," I say, feeling a little silly. "It's not a big deal."

"Maybe Mr. Rupert's an awkward kind of person," she offers. "Some people are so smart but they're not great with people, you know?"

"Maybe," I say thoughtfully.

"I'm here if you need to talk about it or if something else comes up, okay?"

I nod as she pushes away from her desk and comes over to me. "I meant to tell you, I got you a little something." She moves some papers on her desk around and uncovers a small package.

"What is it?" I ask.

"Open it and see," she says, smiling.

I pull open the packaging to find a special lens that attaches to my phone's camera so that I can take better pictures.

"I can't believe you got it!" I say, giving her a big hug.

"Try this one out," she says. "If you like it, and if you can keep up with it for a little while, we can think about getting you a real camera."

I've been trying to convince her to let me get a digital camera since the beginning of the school year. I love taking pictures with my phone and then making artwork out of them on my tablet. I add filters and animations to everyday things like flowers and trees and birds' nests. Sometimes Mom lets me upload the pictures and I get a photo book in the mail a few days later. I made one for Cedrick's dads for their last anniversary and they both cried.

I give my mom another hug and run to show Jules and Cedrick, who are on the couch in the basement. I grab my phone and clip on the little lens, setting the timer for ten seconds, then dive-bomb into the couch, holding the phone at arm's length.

"Get close," I say. "I want some pictures of us for my next photo book."

Cedrick scrambles over and Jules puts their arms around us. I smile, trying to be as cute as possible. Cedrick rolls his eyes back until the only thing I can see is the white part. Jules pushes their long brown hair behind their shoulder and blows a kiss. The flash goes off and we crowd in to look at the screen. It's the best picture I've ever taken with my phone. Every detail is sharp and clear, right down to a booger in Cedrick's left nostril.

"Yikes," he says, covering his face.

"You might wanna handle that," Jules says.

Cedrick turns to me. "We're deleting it, right?"

I hold my phone away from him. "Nope."

"Oh c'mon, Boog! I got a whole booger in my nose!"

"It's perfect," I say.

Cedrick goes to the bathroom and comes back a few minutes later, booger free and still salty that I won't delete the picture. I help Jules with their math homework and they help me with my social studies assignment.

Cedrick quotes *Black Panther* lines until we're sick of him and then my dad orders pizza. After we're all stuffed, my dad walks everyone home while I wait on the porch and then he locks up because my mom is working late.

He kisses me good night and retreats to his man cave. After I brush my teeth, stretch a bonnet over my braids, and climb into bed, I lie awake looking at the ceiling. I'm not feeling sleepy at all so I grab my phone and scroll through my pictures until I get to the one of me, Jules, and Ced. One of the things we learn about vampires is that they don't show up in mirrors and since camera lenses are basically super-sophisticated mirrors, they don't show up in pictures either.

A vamp could've been aggressively break-dancing right behind us and we never would've known.

It suddenly feels too hot to sleep. I set my phone on the bedside table and kick away the blankets to try and find a cool spot in the sheets. When that doesn't work, I slip on my fuzzy house shoes and tiptoe downstairs to get a glass of water.

It's quiet except for the hum of the AC and the never-ending cry of cicadas from outside. In the kitchen I pull a glass out of the cabinet. Just as I set it in the front of the fridge and switch on the little light over the water dispenser, I hear my dad's voice from the basement. He says my name in a way that makes me stop. He calls me Malika and that means whatever it is—it's serious. I put my glass on the counter and quietly creep to the top of the basement steps, leaning down just enough to hear him a little clearer.

"Sam, she's smart. She's just like you. If something comes up and we have to tell her, I think she'll be able to handle it." I don't know what he's talking about but there's something in his voice that makes me a little worried. He almost sounds sad. "It's been so long since we've had to do that. We have to try harder to—"

My curiosity carries me forward and I ease onto the top step. It creaks under my weight.

"That you, Boog?" my dad calls.

I back away from the top of the stairs. "Just getting some water. It's hot upstairs."

"I'll put the AC up a little, okay, baby? Try to get some sleep."

"Okay, Dad." I hold as still as possible because I'm extremely nosy and I want him to continue his conversation.

He stays quiet. He's clearly waiting for me to walk away and now that I've blown my cover, I guess I'll take my behind to bed. I don't hear his voice again as I climb the stairs and go back to my room.

CHAPTER 3

Friday finally rolls around and in Mrs. Lambert's class, she dims the lights and puts on a video explaining the school dress code and other rules that we, according to Ms. Mason, need reminding of. Some girls have been showing off their shoulders a little too much for our district's liking and now we have to talk about how wearing a tank top and shorts above the knee in ninety-degree weather is somehow unacceptable. I make up my mind to organize a protest because first of all, not everybody is just a boy or a girl. You'd think people as ancient as Ms. Mason and her district buddies would learn something new every once in a while. Second, if guys can show off their ashy chicken legs and three armpit hairs when they wear basketball shorts and muscle shirts, everybody else should be able to, too.

The classroom door creaks open and the school secretary,

Mr. Hansen, steps in with a kid wearing a bright orange backpack. The poor kid looks like he's being held hostage. It must be his first day.

Mrs. Lambert has a quiet conversation with Mr. Hansen before directing the kid to an empty seat right next to me and Jules. He sits and stares down at the desk like he's afraid to move.

Jules leans over to him. "Hi. Are you new?" Jules is the unofficial welcoming committee for homeroom. They're always the first person to say hi when new kids come in. This kid is lucky Jules didn't know they were coming ahead of time or there would have been a welcome poster.

The new kid nods. "I—I just moved here. It's my first day."

"You all will have plenty of time to chitchat after class," Mrs. Lambert says, throwing us a pointed glance that melts into a friendly smile. "We have to get through this terrible presentation so please pay attention."

The narrator rambles on and on about the dress code and I roll my eyes so many times I'm actually starting to get a headache.

When it's finally over, we gather up our stuff and head to our second period classes. The new kid stays behind, probably at Mrs. Lambert's request so she can get him up to speed on everything he needs to do.

I meet Jules and Cedrick in the lunchroom after PE. "The gym smells terrible," I say as we sit down with our trays.

"Somebody threw up while we were running laps and Coach told us to just go around."

"Thanks," says Cedrick, looking down at his chili. "Now I can't eat."

"Sorry," I say.

Jules nudges me and I follow their gaze. The new kid is standing off to the side of the lunchroom with his tray in his hands, scanning the crowd. He still looks nervous. Jules is up and zigzagging their way through the crowd before I can say anything. They go over to him and steer him toward our table.

"This is Aaron," says Jules. "Him and his mom just moved here from Colorado and guess where they live? Right at the end of our street!"

"What are you? A detective?" Cedrick asks. "You got all that information in the ten seconds it took you to walk over here."

Jules, with their mouth full of braces and eyes full of kindness, grins. "I'm just friendly. You should try it, Ced."

Aaron sits down. He looks a little less nervous now. I can't imagine what it's like to have to be in a new place with new people, and right in the middle of the year, too. I've had Cedrick and Jules with me since kindergarten and can't imagine going through the school year without them.

"I'm Malika," I say. "Everybody calls me Boog."

"Except when she's in trouble," Jules cuts in.

"They're right. I'm all seven syllables of my full name when I mess up but I'm mostly a good kid, I swear."

Aaron laughs a little. He's a few inches taller than Jules, big brown eyes, a dimple in his left cheek. It's his quiet demeanor that throws me a little. The last new kid we got had a speech and an entire interpretive dance prepared on their first day. I almost died of secondhand embarrassment.

"You met Jules," I say. "They're the welcoming committee. And this is Cedrick. He's the rude one."

"I'm not rude," says Cedrick, sulking.

Maybe rude isn't the right word. He's protective of our little group and sometimes that comes across as him having an attitude. I tease him about it but I know there isn't anything he wouldn't do for me or Jules and I love him like a brother for it.

"Thanks for letting me sit with you," Aaron says. He stares straight down at his tray. "I don't know anybody here."

"Well, now you know us," says Jules. "We're not so bad."

Aaron is so quiet, and I can't tell if that's the way he always is, or if he just needs some time to warm up but he cracks a toothy smile as Cedrick and Jules joke about Mr. Rupert's gleaming bald head and permanent scowl.

"Speaking of Mr. Rupert," Jules says, glancing past me, their eyes narrow.

I turn to see him standing in the cafeteria doorway. When he spots me, he makes a beeline straight toward our table. I duck down, trying to somehow make myself invisible.

"Why is he coming over here?" Aaron asks.

Cedrick shrugs and Aaron looks back and forth between

me and Jules but we don't have an answer either. Mr. Rupert walks up to our table and stares down at me, his eyebrows pushed together.

"Good afternoon." He glances at Aaron. "You're new."

"So are you," I say.

Jules giggles but Mr. Rupert huffs.

"Did we do something wrong?" Cedrick asks. "Not tryna be rude, but you've been following us around."

"That's true," Mr. Rupert admits. "It's my job to know about you all."

He's making the same point as my mom and I guess he's right. Maybe.

"I'm the guidance counselor," Mr. Rupert says to Aaron. "If you need anything, you know where to find me. Moving to a new school can be hard. I'm here if you need to talk."

Mr. Rupert is smiling but I'm 100 percent sure it's fake. He looks like he has to force himself to do it and I'm even more confused about what his problem is. He walks away and as he leaves the cafeteria, Mrs. Lambert smiles politely at him, then finds me in the crowd. She rolls her eyes and points at Mr. Rupert when he turns his back, shaking her head. Even she thinks he's kind of annoying.

"What's his deal?" Aaron asks.

"I think Ms. Mason told him how I like to organize protests against stuff like this," I say, holding up my bowl of chili that smells way too much like dog food for me to eat it. I think about my notes on the dress code video. Now that I think about it, that actually might be the reason Mr. Rupert is sticking his nose in my business. Ms. Mason probably told Mr. Rupert to keep an eye on me. To her, I'm a troublemaker, but almost always good trouble. Mr. Rupert isn't going to stop me from asking questions about our school's outdated rules and he isn't going to keep me from demanding to know the nutritional value of dog-food-flavored chili.

I turn to Aaron, trying to put my thoughts elsewhere. "So, my parents are having a BBQ tonight. Wanna come?"

"We're all going," says Jules.

"You like banana pudding?" Cedrick asks as if it's the only thing that really matters.

Aaron nods. "I have to ask my mom but I don't think we're doing anything anyways."

"Okay," I say, smiling. "Want to give me your phone number so I can text you the address? If you live on Noble Knight, we're right at the end of the cul-de-sac."

I try to think of the last time we had anybody our age come to one of our cookouts. It's always just been me, Jules, and Cedrick, and all our families. It feels kind of nice to invite somebody new over.

The bell rings. I quickly put Aaron's number in my phone and me and Jules go to our afternoon classes in A building while Cedrick and Aaron head to building B. The rest of the day drags on and on until finally, the last bell rings. I practically run out of the building and meet everyone at the bike rack, including Aaron.

"It's the weekend!" Cedrick shouts as he straps on his helmet. "I can't wait to eat, sleep, and watch *Spider-Man*."

"The Miles Morales one?" Aaron asks.

Cedrick's face lights up. He loves that movie more than *Black Panther* and that's sayin' something. "Is there any other version that counts?" he asks, beaming.

Aaron shakes his head. "Not really."

The way they look at each other lets me know things are about to get real nerdy, real fast. Cedrick has fifty-leven theories about the MCU multiverse and while me and Jules love those movies, we're not as into it as he is. But the way him and Aaron start going back and forth tells me he just found someone he can pour his little superhero-loving heart out to, and I love that for him.

"Let's go to my house and help get ready for the BBQ," I say. I glance at Aaron. "Do you have a bike?"

"I do, but the movers haven't brought all our stuff yet."

"That's okay," says Jules. "Hop on the back." They stand on their petals, leaving the seat open for Aaron.

"You sure?" he asks skeptically.

Jules smiles wide and then looks at me. "Y'all better tell him. I can carry any one of you."

"I mean, they can carry you," I say. "But they can also drop you. I got a scar on my knee to prove it."

"Hey!" Jules shouts. "Don't tell him that. You're gonna scare him." They turn to Aaron. "She fell off because we were goin' way too fast down a hill and there was gravel on the road and—you know what? Just hop on and try not to move around too much. I won't let you fall. Promise."

Aaron hesitates for a moment, then gets on the bike and wraps his arms firmly around Jules's waist.

"If we fall over just remember to tuck and roll," says Jules. "Protect your head and neck."

A strangled yelp escapes Aaron's lips as Jules takes off, Aaron clinging to their waist for dear life.

I hop on my bike and me and Cedrick follow Jules across the field behind the school, taking the shortcut. Once again, Mr. Rupert is standing by the gate. Jules quickly pedals past him but as I follow Cedrick through, Mr. Rupert steps onto the narrow path in front of me. I have to grip my brakes—hard—and drag my feet on the ground to keep from running into him.

"You should be more careful," Mr. Rupert says.

"I should be more careful?" I ask, my heart thudding in my chest. "You stepped right in front of me."

"Shortcuts are off the beaten path," Mr. Rupert says, his gaze wandering to the gate. "You should stick to the main sidewalks where there are lots of other people."

I want to tell him to mind his business but choose my words a little more carefully.

"You don't need to worry about me. My parents know I go this way."

His eyebrows shoot up like he's shocked. "Do they now?"

Cedrick and Jules—with Aaron teetering on the seat of the bike—stop on the other side of the gate.

"Come on, Boog," Cedrick calls. "No talking to strangers, remember?"

Mr. Rupert shoots Cedrick an angry glance. He steps aside and I peddle past him.

"He's such a creep," Jules says as we hurry down the side street.

"I don't get it," I say. I'm thinking about bringing it up to my mom again as we turn onto Noble Knight Road.

"Right here," Aaron says.

His house is the big gray one with the white trim right at the beginning of our street. I didn't know the people who lived there before and the place has been empty for a while. There are just six houses between Aaron's and mine and I take that as a little bit of a sign that we're supposed to be friends.

"You can come in," Aaron says. "We don't have much, like I said, the movers haven't brought all our stuff yet. We're sleeping on air mattresses and living off pizza and Whataburger right now."

"Oh man, Whataburger," Cedrick says like he can almost taste it. "It's been so long . . ."

"Oh my god, Cedrick," Jules says. "Please get it together.

You're about to start drooling and then Aaron's not gonna want to be friends with you."

Cedrick straightens up and smooths out his shirt. "I could eat a whole cow right now."

We leave our bikes on the sidewalk and trudge up the walkway. Aaron's front lawn is a mess and I know that as soon as my mom and Jules's mom get a look at it, they'll be over here offering to fix it up like they had for Cedrick's dads. It'll be mostly Jules's mom, though. My mom has a tendency to kill plants on contact.

Aaron walks up to the front door and takes out his house key but before he gets a chance to put it in the lock, the door swings open and a tall woman in gray sweats, her braids piled on top of her head, a yellow headscarf securing them in place, stands in the doorway.

"Hey, Mom," Aaron says.

The woman wraps him up and kisses the top of his head. "Making friends already?" she asks as she looks us over.

"Hi!" Jules says, pushing their way between me and Cedrick. "I'm Jules. It's nice to meet you."

"Hi, baby," Aaron's mom says warmly. She's got the same gentle personality as Aaron. They look just alike, too.

"Mom, this is Malika but we all call her Boog," says Aaron, smiling at me. "That's Cedrick and you met Jules already."

"Wonderful," Aaron's mom says, smiling. "I'm Kim. I'm so happy Aaron's got some friends already. Come on in and make yourselves at home."

"This house is so nice, Miss Kim," says Jules as they look around. "It's been empty for a little while, right?"

"It has," says Miss Kim. "Probably because they wanted way too much money for it but my negotiating skills came in pretty handy." She walks into the big open kitchen and looks around inside the fridge. "I've got some junk y'all can have. My only rule is that you clean up after yourselves."

Cedrick smiles wide. "Yes, ma'am."

Miss Kim sets a bunch of sodas and chips and a stack of ramen on the counter. "Help yourselves. When the movers bring the rest of the kitchen stuff I'll have y'all over for a real dinner."

We all grab noodles and Aaron's mom heats up a pot of water on the stove, apologizing for not having a microwave yet. I nudge Aaron's shoulder and mouth the word "BBQ" to him.

"Oh right," he says quietly. "Hey, Mom, Boog's parents are having a BBQ tonight. Can we go?"

Miss Kim turns and gives him a look. It's the don't-ask-me-for-stuff-in-front-of-people look. Like when I want Jules or Cedrick to stay over and I ask my mom right in front of them, there's a better chance she'll say yes because she loves my friends but she presses her lips together real tight and narrows her eyes at me while she's saying yes.

"We don't have plans so I guess that'd be fine," she says. "Are you sure it's okay with your parents?"

"Oh yes, ma'am." As I say the words, I'm actually not 100 percent sure.

We celebrated Jules's mom's birthday in their backyard and 'Lita cooked and we all sang karaoke. We had a huge thing for Cedrick's dad when he got promoted and I think some of his coworkers were there, too, but I can't remember for sure. It's rarely anyone other than just us and our families but Aaron and his mom are new around here. Inviting them is the polite thing to do.

"I'll bring a fruit tray," Miss Kim says. "What time should we head over?"

"Five," I say a little nervously. Aaron and I are going to be friends. I can already tell. And the way him and Cedrick were excitedly discussing Miles Morales makes me happy in a way I didn't know I could be. I never needed anybody besides Jules and Ced. But maybe that was because it has always been just us. My parents can't be mad that I want to let new people into our circle, especially people as nice as Aaron and his mom.

I picture my mom giving me that same look Miss Kim had just given Aaron. I need to let her know that we'll have extra guests and I hope she won't be too mad that I invited them.

CHAPTER 4

We finish our snacks and say goodbye to Aaron and his mom
before hopping back on our bikes and riding to the end of the
cul-de-sac. I run into the house, kick off my shoes, and find
my mom in the kitchen. She and my dad are slow dancing to
some old music she's playing on her phone.

I quickly squeeze in between them. "No dancing without
me. I have to make sure y'all don't attempt anything too risky.
Two-steppin' only, please."

My mom shoos me away. "Girl, stop. Me and your dad
don't get a chance to go out much anymore. This is as close as
we're gonna get."

"I still got it," my dad says as he twirls my mom in a circle.

"You sure do," she says.

"I—I think I want to throw up," I say dramatically.

"Well, don't do it in my kitchen," my mom says. "Everything is clean and we're about to set up outside."

I turn and try to slink away but my mom catches me by the arm and spins me around.

"And you're just in time to help," she says, smiling. "Are Jules and Cedrick with you?" She peers around me and spots them in the entryway. "Why don't y'all go set up the lawn chairs and turn on the lights."

"What kind of food are you making, Mrs. Wilson?" Cedrick asks.

"Tre's putting ribs on the grill, and chicken, too, I think," she says.

Cedrick and Jules exchange excited glances.

Me and Jules help set up the lawn chairs in the backyard. I turn on the length of fairy lights my mom has strung through the wooden slats that cover the back porch. Cedrick helps my dad put potato chips in big plastic bowls and fills the coolers with ice so the sodas and bottled waters stay cold. I use my new lens and snap pictures of Cedrick making funny faces and Jules posing against the backdrop of twinkling lights.

At four thirty, my dad changes into his new sandals, a polo shirt, and an apron that says Kiss the Chef across the front. He slides a pair of metal tongs into the front pocket like it's his weapon of choice in a battle with BBQ chicken and grilled corn. He carries a tray of seasoned ribs and chicken legs outside.

My mom brings him a big plate piled high with hot dogs

and hamburgers that he throws on the grate. I move around to get a better angle and snap a picture of them. Dad raises his tongs in the air and clicks them together and Mom puckers her lips and plants a kiss on his cheek. As I zoom in to take another one, my mom's expression shifts. Her gaze wanders out over the Green and her brow furrows. At first I think maybe she sees something beyond the back fence but when I follow her gaze all I see is the sky turning fiery orange as the sun prepares to set. When I turn back to her, she leans in close to my dad, her voice low.

"We should have started the party a little earlier," she says. "I don't like being out here this late."

I glance at Jules but they haven't noticed what she said or more importantly, the *way* she said it. She's worried. Not just worried. Scared. All because we're in our own backyard a little too close to sunset.

My dad gives her a quick kiss. "It's all right. We'll cook, then move everything inside."

Of all the little things my parents do that irk me, this one isn't as annoying as it is sad. We're in our own yard, surrounded by people we know. There's literally nothing to be afraid of and still, she's on edge every time the shadows start to creep in. I don't fully understand what it must have been like for her to grow up under the constant threat of a vampire attack but I know it's why she has such a hard time letting those fears go.

The doorbell rings. My mom puts on a smile and hurries to the front door. "I got it," she says. "It's Celia and Lidia."

Jules and Cedrick follow me inside as my mom opens the door and the three of them immediately start cackling and joking and talking about their day. They haul in all the dishes 'Lita has prepared and the smell of all the delicious food wafts through the air. Cedrick motions for me and Jules to follow him into the front room.

"How long do ribs take to cook?" he asks.

I shrug. "A little while but the chicken should be done quick."

"I'm so hungry," Cedrick says. "I could eat a whole pig. My dad better not try to tell me I can't have meat today."

"Or what?" Jules asks, teasing Cedrick a little. "What are you gonna do if he does?"

Cedrick opens his mouth, then closes it. He thinks. "I mean probably just cry alone in my room, but—you know what?" He pauses and takes a deep breath. "Whatever, Jules. I'm eating pigs and cows and chickens today. Nobody is gonna stop me. I'm done with this plant stuff."

Cedrick is gonna eat lettuce and ice cubes if that's what his dad tells him to do but I'm positive tonight will be an exception. There's just too much good stuff laid out.

The doorbell rings again and my mom runs over to open it. Cedrick's dads come in carrying more drinks and more trays of food. I spot a glass serving dish with Nilla Wafers pressed up against the inside and the yellow pudding Cedrick's dad, Mr. Ethan, makes from scratch oozing through.

"Want me to carry that for you, Mr. Ethan?" I ask.

He smiles warmly. "I don't think so, Boog. The banana pudding might not make it to the kitchen intact."

"I mean, you're not wrong," I say jokingly. "You can't blame me for wanting to eat dessert first when you make the banana pudding."

"True," he says, giving me a big hug. "But your mama would probably chop me in the throat."

"I might," my mom chimes in.

"Let's not test her," Mr. Ethan says, smiling. "I need to show you this roast, Sam." He sets down a glass tray and peels back the foil lid to reveal a big chunk of meat that's been tied together with string. The fancy little loops sit atop the browned roast and the smell coming off it makes my mouth water.

"It's too pretty to eat," my mom says. She gives Mr. Ethan a wink and covers the tray.

"Ced," I say. "Your dad made real meat."

Cedrick looks like he's gonna cry. Someone switches on the music and I plop down on the couch as Jules grabs Cedrick's hand and pulls him in to the most awkward dance routine I've ever seen. Jules is good but Cedrick can't keep up and soon falls into the couch next to me with a heavy sigh.

"I give up," he says. "I only know the dances they teach us in gym."

"They still got y'all learning dances in PE?" my dad asks as he buzzes around the dining room table putting out stacks of plates and napkins. "What is it? The electric slide?"

"I don't know what that is, Mr. Wilson," Cedrick says. "Is that what y'all learned back in olden times?"

"Olden times?" My dad looks like he might crumble into a pile of dust. "I was born in '78, sir."

"Did they have cars back then?" Jules asks.

My dad throws his hands up and marches into the kitchen. "Somebody get these kids. They makin' me feel old."

Me and Jules grin at each other.

I get up and take Cedrick's place. Me and Jules dance like we're auditioning to be one of Beyoncé's backup dancers. Auditioning and failing, but we laugh until we can't breathe. The doorbell rings again. But this time my parents' chatter stops midsentence. The music suddenly cuts out.

"Expecting someone?" Jules's mom asks. There's something in her voice that makes me nervous.

I look down at the floor, my heart thudding. This is my fault. It's gotta be Aaron and his mom but I got caught up in getting ready and forgot to tell my mom they were coming.

The mood in the room shifts from singing and dancing and laughing to something heavy and serious. I catch my dad and Jules's mom glancing out the window and then turning their attention back to us.

"Malika," my mom says. She's using my real name and I already know I'm in trouble.

I scramble to explain. "I—I asked my friend Aaron and his mom to come over. They live right down the street. They're new and he's in my homeroom class and I thought—"

"What did you say to them?" my mom asks, crossing the room and standing in front of me. She's angrier than I've seen her in a long time. "Word for word—what did you say?"

"I asked Aaron if he wanted to come to the BBQ and he asked his mom if they could come over. She said yes and—"

"Did you tell them they could come in?" she asks, cutting me off. Her voice is flat, eyes narrow.

"No." I know better than that but right then, I realize how bad I messed up.

It's universally understood that vampires had to be invited in order to gain access to a place where humans lived. Nobody really knows why, but what we learn in school is that the threshold of a dwelling represents a kind of barrier that a vamp can't cross unless they are invited to do so. There are lots of stories about vampires trying to muscle their way into dwellings only to burst into flames. I've heard other things, too. An uninvited vamp might begin to bleed from every orifice all at once.

But vampires were known to be highly intelligent. They could change their outward appearances long enough to assume the form of some harmless postal worker or pizza delivery person and had been able to trick people into letting them in. It was for that exact reason people had made rules to protect themselves. Never invite anyone in.

I glance at my dad but his gaze is darting around the room—to the basement door, to the bookshelf, and then back to me. My mom draws her mouth into a tight line, closes her eyes for a quick second, then turns to Dad. She lifts her chin slightly. Everyone suddenly shifts. Dad pulls Jules and Cedrick into the kitchen, telling them he needs help with something, which is a lie, but they do as they're told. My mom nudges me toward the couch. She makes eye contact with Cedrick's dad and he goes to the door.

Mom hoists a cooler full of drinks onto her hip and takes a deep breath. She nods and Cedrick's dad pulls the door open. Aaron and his mom stand on the other side. The cooler suddenly slips from my mom's grip and hits the ground with a loud crash, sending cans of soda and bottled water rolling in all directions. Ice cubes scatter across the tile in the entryway and Aaron and his mom both rush in and start scooping up the drinks.

I hear my dad exhale between his teeth. Everything snaps back into action. The music comes back on and 'Lita helps Aaron's mom collect the rest of the drinks.

"I couldn't keep hold of it," my mom says cheerfully. "Sorry, y'all."

It's been a while, but I've seen my parents do this routine before. It isn't often we have uninvited guests but it does happen and they have little routines like this one that they use to keep everybody safe. Aaron and his mom had stepped right over the threshold without a second thought so they passed that test; they weren't vampires. If they had been, they'd be charred piles of dust by now. I could feel the heat rising in my face. I was going to have to explain to Aaron that my parents refuse to let go of the old way of doing things and I dread having to have that conversation.

I creep to the entryway and avoid my mom's gaze. "Mom, this is Aaron and his mom, Miss Kim."

My mom shakes Miss Kim's hand and calls my dad over. As they get acquainted, I nudge Aaron toward the kitchen, putting some distance between me and my parents. I know I'm gonna be in trouble for inviting them over without asking, but I'm hoping they'll wait till later to talk to me about it.

"You made it," I say.

Aaron smiles and looks down at the floor.

Jules comes over and puts their arm around my shoulder. "Sorry our parents are so weird. They're old school."

Aaron looks confused. I shake my head, embarrassed.

"We don't have to get into it," Aaron says softly, nudging my shoulder with his. "So, what's the plan? We brought a fruit tray."

I'm so happy he's not going to press me about my parents, for a split second I forget how much trouble I'm going to be in later. "Food, maybe some games, then a movie?" I look between Cedrick and Jules, who nod.

"Can we go outside?" Cedrick calls to his dad, who's taken a seat on the couch.

"Sure," Mr. Ethan answers.

My mom mutters something under her breath as we go out the back door. 'Lita follows close behind and sits in a deck chair, sipping lemonade and watching us like a hawk.

Soon, Cedrick's dad and my dad are following us out the back door as they joke about my dad's new sandals and he tells them he's convinced my mom did something to his other pair. I have to walk away so he doesn't catch me laughing.

My mom comes out to the backyard, laughing and chatting with Aaron's mom. They seem to have hit it off, which catches me a little off guard. Our parents are a lot like us. They keep their circle small but seeing her with Miss Kim is actually really nice.

"Is everybody here always so jumpy when y'all have company?" Aaron asks. "It's the threshold thing, isn't it?"

Me and Jules whip our heads around to stare at him.

"You don't have to be embarrassed," Aaron says. "My grandma didn't stop vamp-proofing her house until I was, like, five. I get it."

A rush of relief washes over me. He understands. At least a little, and if that's true, then it's probably better to get it all out in the open. I don't know how to explain it to him in a way that doesn't sound ridiculous but if I don't tell him the truth he might hear it from someone at school. I picture Adrianna cornering him and telling him a bunch of lies and then I'd have to fight her. Not that I've ever actually been in a fight but I feel like I can take her. Her giant forehead probably makes her unsteady on her feet. I picture Aaron walking away from us, treating us like half the kids in school and it makes my stomach ache. I'll do anything to avoid that even if it means letting him in on the embarrassing stuff our parents do.

"Our parents are—protective," I say.

Aaron raises an eyebrow. "What do you mean?"

Jules sighs and Cedrick just shakes his head and shoves his hands in his pockets.

"They just have a hard time letting stuff go," I say. "They still do some things that people used to do before the Reaping."

"But they don't actually believe we still have to worry about vamps, right?" Aaron asks.

I realize I've never really thought about it like that. Our parents use vampire-proof cleaner and are a little jumpy in the nighttime hours but it's because old habits die hard. It's because they have a hard time letting the past go.

"Everybody knows vampires are extinct now," I say. "But our parents grew up in a time when there were still a few vampires left, including the San Antonio hive. That was obviously a long time ago but, I don't know. I can't really blame them for being a little more careful than other people."

Cedrick nods. "And if you add in the fact that 'Lita was there at the Reaping and she—"

"Wait. What?" Aaron is completely blindsided by this little bit of information. A part of me hopes he thinks it's cool but another part of me wishes Cedrick hadn't even said anything at all. "She—she's a Vanquisher?"

"She was," I say quietly.

"Good job, Cedrick." Jules scowls. "We're supposed to try and keep that quiet."

Cedrick shrugs. "Everybody already knows. You'd think it'd make us more popular at school but she won't even come up there to make us look good."

"Because she's over it," Jules says. "She wants to leave the past alone, too."

"Does she?" Cedrick asks. "Then why does she keep making that homemade repellent? Why is she always watching us like a vamp is gonna swoop in and snap our necks off?"

"Snap our necks off?" I ask. "Ced, that's not even what they did." He's so dramatic. Aaron turns to look for 'Lita but she's disappeared somewhere inside. I put my hand on Aaron's shoulder. "She's actually really nice," I say.

He can't even fix his mouth to respond and I laugh a little.

"Anyway," Cedrick continues, sounding a little annoyed. "They know vamps are history but all the never-invite-anybody-in rules and the homemade repellent that smells like sweaty armpits, it's like a bad habit. Like biting your nails or picking your nose or something."

Might as well put it all out there and let Aaron decide if he's going to be a total jerk, like Adrianna, or maybe, hopefully, he'll choose to be something else.

"We can't be out after dark," I say. "We don't buy store-brand repellent because they don't trust it to work. And as you saw, our parents are a little weird about inviting people in. It's not like we're carrying stakes and holy water."

I avoid Aaron's gaze for a moment but when I finally work up the nerve to look at him, he's smiling in the softest, kindest way.

"My mom still vampire-proofs things," he says.

Cedrick and Jules whip their heads around to stare at him and a little flutter of hope settles in my stomach. He's even more like us than I'd thought.

"It's how her mom raised her even though my grandma never saw a real vampire in the flesh," Aaron says. "She's not strict about stuff. She only uses vampire repellent every once in a while."

A clatter of plates startles me. My dad has knocked a plate off the small table next to the grill. He's furiously turning the chicken legs and checking them with the meat thermometer, glancing over at us and then to Cedrick's dad, who looks up at the sky, then looks at us, too.

"Why don't y'all come inside and we'll play a game or something?" he says.

"We're good, Dad," Cedrick calls back.

Cedrick's dad and my dad exchange glances.

"Inside," my dad says. He's not upset but there's an edge to his voice. "Charades and blindfolded Pictionary sound like a good time."

He's not asking, he's telling. So, we all trudge inside while my dad finishes up the food and hauls everything in.

Jules and Aaron sit with me in the little seat in front of the bay window in the living room. My mom blindfolds 'Lita and she tries to draw something on the Pictionary board. It looks like an elephant with wings and human feet. Aaron laughs himself to tears and Cedrick has to tip his head back so juice doesn't shoot out his nose when we all give up and she tells us it was supposed to be Pegasus.

I take my turn, drawing a giraffe so terrible Cedrick thinks it's a dalmatian and Jules thinks it's a cow. After we play all the games and eat more banana pudding than any human being should, Cedrick and his dads head home with Jules, their mom and grandma following behind. My mom offers to walk Aaron and his mom home.

"We're okay," says Miss Kim. "Thank you so much for having us."

She and my mom give each other a hug, like they actually really like each other, and I wonder if maybe my mom needs some new people in her circle as much as I do. Maybe some of Miss Kim's easygoing attitude will rub off on her.

"Text me tomorrow," I tell Aaron as I walk him to the

door. "I think we're going to do a movie night." We're supposed to be over at Ced's tonight but I know better than to even ask at this point.

"I'm in," he says.

Mom and Miss Kim are in the process of exchanging numbers when my dad sets his hands on my shoulders.

"Why don't you go brush your teeth and get to bed," he says quietly. "Let me talk to your mom for a minute."

I hit the stairs before he has a chance to change his mind. I brush my teeth, tuck my braids under a jumbo-sized bonnet, and slide into bed. I hear the front door close and the water turn on in the kitchen, the clang of dishes and my mom's hushed voice. Suddenly I hear footsteps on the stairs and shut my eyes, pretending to be asleep.

My door creaks open. I take long slow breaths and hold still.

"You're a terrible actress," Mom says, sitting down on the edge of my bed. "I'm upset and I want to talk to you about it."

I roll over and sit up. "I know I messed up."

She stares at me and shakes her head. "No. I messed up. I think I embarrassed you."

I shrug. "Maybe a little. I'm sorry. I know I should've asked before I invited Aaron and Miss Kim over."

"That's true," she says. "But the way we reacted was—not great. I know we do things a little different but that is no excuse."

"I haven't seen you and Daddy act like that about guests in a really long time."

She sighs and looks down into her lap. "I know. I haven't been so hung up on uninvited guests since you were in kindergarten. You probably don't even remember but I used to have our mail go to a PO box. Anytime I ordered something I'd track it down to the hour so that nobody could pop up on us unexpectedly." She laughs lightly. "I never even used to order pizza. I'd always just go pick it up."

I stare into her face. "I don't remember any of that."

"Good," she says. "I'm a little embarrassed myself. I just love you and Daddy so much."

"I know," I said. "And you like Aaron's mom, right? I know I should've asked but you're glad they came over, right?"

"They seem like good people," she says. "But next time, make sure you ask. You just never know and it could've been dangerous and—" She stops short. Like she's said too much. "I don't even know how to say it."

"Say what?" I ask. I put my hand on hers and she smiles gently but her eyes look sad.

"I know that other people have been letting their guard down since the Reaping but, Boog, baby, you weren't there. You don't know what it's like to hear the stories and live under the threat of those monsters every day. No matter how small the hives were or how small the threat seemed, it was life or death for us at one point." Her eyes mist over and she lowers her voice. "I'd do anything to keep you safe and if that means I take some extra, maybe even unnecessary precautions— well—I can live with that. I'll try not to go overboard, though. Deal?"

"Deal," I say.

"There's nothing to be afraid of anymore, Boog," she says. "But we still have to be careful. Just in case."

"In case what?" I ask.

She leans in close to me and kisses me on the forehead. "In case your mama is just a little too stuck in her ways. Give me some time, baby."

"Am I in trouble for inviting Aaron and Miss Kim over without asking?" I'm hoping this conversation means I'm not.

She smiles. "Maybe not. Let me sleep on it."

I think it's the first time I've heard her admit that she knows what she's doing is a little silly. It makes me wonder about the future. Maybe, just maybe, there's a real chance I can do the things all the other kids get to do—going out after sunset, running to the car to grab my bag or check the mail, sitting out under the night sky to watch the stars. I want that so much.

Mom tucks me in, then cuts off the light on her way out. As I lie in the dark, I wonder what it might be like to not have this worry hanging over us all the time. Would it feel different? Would it change us?

A thin sliver of moonlight shines through a crack in the

curtains. It's the only light in my darkened room but it's enough to make shadows of the chair at my desk, the closet door, even my fan as it spins over my head. A shiver runs up my back. I pull the covers up to my neck and start to wonder if it's not just my parents who need to learn to let the past go.

There's nothing to be afraid of anymore, Boog.

CHAPTER 5

I don't do anything all weekend except help my dad clean out the garage. My parents don't tell me I'm on punishment but they don't let Jules, Cedrick, or Aaron come over at all. I start a new group text and add everyone to it. Jules is the first to respond.

JULES: My mom and 'Lita have me doing way too many chores

CEDRICK: Me and my dad are making brownies

ME: Jules, I'm sorry, boo. Ced, I need you to bring me seven brownies ASAP

JULES: ☹

CEDRICK: LOL

AARON: Me and my mom are at the park but there's like six racoons eating out of a trash can. I hate it here.

Everybody's busy and I'm bored out of my mind. I toss my phone onto my bed and go find my mom, who tells me she thinks folding laundry is kind of relaxing and I just don't get why she lies to me like that. There's nothing relaxing about folding Daddy's socks and drawers and cleaning baseboards but that's exactly what ends up happening even though I'm not on punishment.

Monday morning in homeroom Mrs. Lambert is going on and on about the importance of checking the online portal to make sure we're not missing any assignments.

"Can't you just tell us if we're missing anything?" Adrianna asks.

"I'm not your mama," Mrs. Lambert says. "If your grade is dropping because you're not turning your work in, then you already know what you need to do."

Adrianna is about to protest when the intercom crackles to life and cuts her off.

"Attention, students!" Ms. Mason always yells her announcements even though everybody can hear her just fine when she uses her inside voice. Mrs. Lambert cups her hands over her ears. "Remember that this weekend is the fundraising event at the Royal Roller Rink," Ms. Mason continues. "This event is only for Victor Garcia Middle School students, staff, and their families. Pizza will be two dollars a slice. Sodas and juice a dollar a piece. All the money will go toward getting new tablets for the library. See you there and please be on your best behavior!"

Cedrick leans over to Aaron. "You going?"

Aaron nods and turns to me. "You?"

"If my parents let me," I say. "They had me in the house all weekend."

Jules huffs loudly. "Me too. You'd think I was in trouble or something."

"You know what my dad did?" Cedrick asks. "He replaced our back door."

"Say what?" I ask, a little confused. "Why?"

Cedrick shrugs. "I don't even know. Wanna guess what the new one is made out of?"

I think for a minute but can't put it together.

"It's made of metal," Cedrick says.

"Like steel?" Jules asks.

Cedrick shakes his head. "No. Like silver."

I stare into Cedrick's face as a million thoughts tumble through my head. Why would he put up a silver door? After everything me and my mom had talked about I worry that now she'll see Ced's dad taking the extra and super-unnecessary step of putting up a vampire-proof door and all the things she said she might ease up on will be out the window.

"Does your pops know something we don't know?" I ask as I slide down in my seat and cross my arms over my chest.

"I don't think so," Cedrick says. "He's just doing what he always does—overreacting and being weird. I don't even know what was wrong with the other door, but he took it off the hinges and put the new one up yesterday at like eight in the morning."

Mrs. Lambert clears her throat loudly. "All that talking must be because the Squad is making plans to get their homework turned in early." She smiles at us and we quickly end our conversation and get to work.

At the end of the day we all meet up at Cedrick's house and sure enough, a silver door is sitting where the old one used to be. It's bulky and ugly and doesn't even have a window in it.

"You all act like you've never seen a door before," Cedrick's dad says as he whips up an after-school snack of grilled cheese sandwiches made with some fancy kind of bread and cheese that I suspect isn't really cheese but some kind of cashew-almond imposter cheese.

"Did something happen to the other door?" I ask.

Cedrick's dad flips over a sandwich and presses it flat in the pan. "This one is more secure. Top-of-the-line silver plating over a steel core. Nothing is getting through there." His gaze wanders off to the side a little, like he's thinking about something real hard. "You can never be too cautious."

My mom cannot hear about this but knowing how tight everybody is, she probably already has and I'm a little salty about it. Just when I think we'll get to leave the vamp stuff behind, here comes a reminder that maybe we shouldn't.

"So, Dad," Cedrick says. "There's a fundraiser at the Royal Roller Rink this weekend. Can we go?"

Cedrick's dad's eyes light up. "Roller skating, huh? You know, I used to be king of the rink when I was in high school."

Cedrick looks down at the table. "Here we go," he says under his breath.

Jules nudges Aaron in the arm and they both smile.

"You won some competitions, right?" I ask him the question but I already know the answer. Cedrick's dad loves to talk about his roller skating past and I think it's hilarious but Cedrick thinks it's embarrassing. He shoots me a sideways glance.

"I didn't just win," says his dad. "I shut it down. Nobody even came close. I could do the snake walk, the iceberg, the toe jam—"

"The toe jam?" Cedrick asks. "Dad, seriously?"

He slides a perfectly browned grilled cheese onto Cedrick's plate. I take a picture of it with my phone to add to my collection of tasty things Cedrick's parents make.

"Boy, stop," says his dad. "We're going to go to this fundraiser and imma show y'all all my moves."

"Now I don't wanna go," Cedrick says, pouting.

"Oh, we're going," says Jules. "No way I'm missing this."

After school the next day, we all meet up with our bikes outside my house. The movers finally delivered Aaron's bike and he's the last one to roll up.

"What are we getting into?" he asks.

"We're gonna cut across the Green and get ice cream at the strip mall on the other side," I say.

"I can't wait!" Cedrick says excitedly.

"Are you even supposed to be eating dairy?" Jules asks. "I thought it was almond milk ice cream only?"

"I don't know what I'm *supposed* to do but I know what I'm gonna do," Cedrick says. "I'm getting a triple-scoop sundae and nobody can stop me."

We take off with Cedrick leading the way. We ride down the block and cut through the neighborhood, across the Green, and up the embankment on the other side.

The Helotes Strip has a movie theater, a nail shop, and a bunch of little stores. It used to be a medical plaza where people could donate blood and plasma but the city shut it down the year before the Reaping. The only signs of what the space had once been used for are solid steel posts that stick up out of the ground every ten feet. A long time ago they were filled with molten silver and acted as an added layer of protection against vamps trying to get inside the blood bank.

The posts are hollow now and we chain our bikes to one poking out of the cracked sidewalk in front of Cold Stone. As we pile in, the girl behind the counter smiles at us.

"Uh-oh," she says playfully. "Here comes trouble."

"Who's trouble?" Cedrick asks. "Don't give us a hard time, Heather. We're not babies anymore."

Heather is in high school and she used to babysit us after school sometimes when we were in the fourth grade.

"You're not babies," Heather says. "But you *are* trouble."

She eyes Aaron. "And I see the Squad has a new member. Does his mama know y'all are trouble?"

"Yup," I say, giving Aaron a gentle nudge.

"What'll it be, Boog?" Heather asks me. "Vanilla in a waffle cone with brownie chunks on top?"

"Yes, ma'am," I say, and then turn to Aaron. "Get whatever you want. My treat. My grandma sends me a whole five dollars on my birthday every year and, like, fifteen at Christmas."

Aaron laughs. "Oh, I didn't know you were ballin'."

Cedrick reaches for my cash and I snatch it away from him. "If you weren't with me when I was broke, you don't get to be with me now that I got, like, twenty-two whole dollars."

"You're still broke and so am I," says Cedrick.

Jules takes out a debit card and hands it to Heather.

"You got a bank card?" Cedrick asks.

Jules grins. "Yup. Mom says I need to learn fiscal responsibility."

Aaron and Cedrick exchange confused glances.

"Uh, what's that mean?" asks Aaron.

"Being responsible with money and stuff," Jules says.

Heather hands me my cone and gets to work on Ced's. "Does buying ice cream for your friends count as being responsible with your money?" she asks.

"Yes," Jules says proudly.

We pay and I slip half my money in Jules's back pocket because they won't let me pay them back. I sit on the little bench outside and Jules squeezes in beside me as Aaron and Ced race to eat their ice cream before it melts. I snap pictures of them stuffing their faces and I get a few cute shots of me and Jules.

"It's, like, a hundred degrees," Jules groans. "Why is the sun like this? It's disrespectful."

"Hey, look," Cedrick says quietly. "It's Mrs. Lambert."

I look across the parking lot and see the back of Mrs. Lambert's head as she disappears into the pet supply store.

"Should we go say hi?" Jules asks.

"No way," Cedrick says. "It's outside of school hours. Nobody wants to see their teachers in the real world. It's weird."

"It's Mrs. Lambert, though," I say. She's our favorite teacher. If it had been that weird old Mr. Rupert I would have said let's get on our bikes and roll out. "Let's say hi."

We toss our napkins in the trash and walk across the lot to the pet store. It's not one of those big chain stores, it's more like a mom-and-pop pet supply place. The building used to be a Chuck E. Cheese. Now, instead of fake rats they house real ones alongside all kinds of other weird creatures. I've only been inside this place once with my dad when he was looking for some food for the fish he used to keep in his office. He said the prices were way too high so we never went back.

We go inside and the smell hits me in the back of my throat. It's like cut grass and dirt and boo boo all rolled into one. I clap my hand over my nose and mouth.

"Ew," Jules says.

"It's funky as heck in here," says Aaron.

Cedrick stifles a laugh.

The air is thick and humid. I can feel the moisture clinging to my skin. It's dark, too, with most of the light emanating from the heat lamps trained on individual glass terrariums filled with lizards and snakes.

The guy behind the counter glances up at us, rolls his eyes, then goes back to reading a Dracula comic.

I glance around and don't see Mrs. Lambert anywhere. The wide center aisle is dotted with freestanding racks of outfits for dogs and plastic chew toys. The shelves to the right and left are mostly food and grooming supplies but toward the back there are rows and rows of fish tanks and cages. I glance down each aisle as we move deeper into the store.

"What do you mean?" I hear Mrs. Lambert's voice somewhere close by. "I thought you said I could get them here."

Jules turns down an aisle and I follow them as Aaron and Cedrick trip along behind me. Near the rear of the store Mrs. Lambert is standing very close to one of the other employees. He's wearing the store's signature green-and-yellow vest and he looks pissed.

"What have you been doing with them?" the guy asks. "I just think it's weird."

"Why don't you mind your own business," Mrs. Lambert snaps. "I just want to buy a few more. My money's not good here or something?"

"No. But I'm just saying, you could use the frozen kind. They don't always have to be live."

Mrs. Lambert takes a step back. "Excuse me?" She sounds absolutely done.

I stop and turn around. "Let's just go," I whisper. "She's pissed about something."

Cedrick nods but as he turns, he runs right into Aaron who rocks to the side and grabs on to a shelf to try and steady himself, but the whole thing comes loose and a stack of plastic food bowls crash to the floor.

Mrs. Lambert spins around. "Malika?" she asks.

Cedrick tries to act like he doesn't see the dozens of bowls still spinning around on the floor and Aaron's face has turned ruddy. Jules grimaces and starts picking up the scattered bowls as Mrs. Lambert walks up to us.

"Hi, Mrs. Lambert," I say quickly. "We—uh—we saw you come in. We wanted to say hi."

The clerk scoots past us and disappears down the aisle. Mrs. Lambert gives him an angry look before turning to me.

"That's nice of you all," she says. She holds a clear plastic bag in her hand. Inside it is a wriggling mass of legs and brown exoskeletons—roaches. I instinctively rear back. When you live in Texas roaches are a thing but I'd never seen so many all in one place.

"For my lizard," she says, giving the bag a little jiggle.

I'm really hoping it's closed up tight. "Oh right. I didn't know you liked reptiles."

She smiles. "Oh yeah. I have two big ones at home. They love these things." She stares at the bag. "Makes me sick, but hey. Gotta do what I gotta do." She peers around at Ced and Jules and Aaron, who've got all the bowls back up on the shelf. "What are y'all up to today?"

"We came to get ice cream," Ced says.

"Sounds like a good idea," says Mrs. Lambert. "I came to get snacks for my lizards and—well I already said that, didn't I?" Mrs. Lamberts suddenly seems flustered. "I gotta run. My babies are probably starving." Again, she shakes the bag of roaches in front of us and we all take a little step back. "Be good. Stay out of trouble."

"We will," I say.

She skirts around us and heads to the counter where she pays and then leaves.

"Since she likes lizards so much, we should ask her if we can have a class pet," Jules says.

"Aht. Aht," Cedrick says. "Remember what happened to Fifi last year in Mrs. Kinsley's class."

"That was an accident," I remind him. "A terrible, awful accident."

"What happened?" asks Aaron.

Jules opens their mouth to speak but Cedrick cuts them off. "Jules, please don't say it. I don't want to cry. Y'all know I loved Fifi."

I lean close to Aaron. "Somebody let Fifi the hamster out of her cage and she got lost. They found her later but it was too late."

"Ohhhhh," Aaron says.

Cedrick's bottom lip quivers and Jules puts their arm around him. "It's okay. Fifi is in a better place."

Cedrick lets Jules steer him out of the pet shop and once we're outside he calms down.

"You're so sensitive," I say. "I think that's the best thing about you, Ced."

He tilts his head back and looks at the sky. "I'll never forget you, Fifi!" he hollers, his voice cracking.

I have to bite the inside of my lip to keep from laughing. My poor Cedrick. He's a mess.

We get our bikes and ride back across the Green. Aaron pats Cedrick on the back after he's had a chance to collect himself and they plan to start a group chat at eight o'clock sharp to discuss their latest rankings of Spider-Man appearances. Me and Jules agree to join but we're not super happy about it.

"See y'all later," I say.

Aaron waves and pedals down the street to his house. I'm in my driveway before I glance back. Aaron is standing on his porch. His head is angled to the side, like he's listening to something. I wave my arms at him. He sees me and waves back before going inside. A little shiver makes its way up my back and settles at the base of my neck. I hurry inside and lock the door.

CHAPTER 6

Sunday night comes quick. I've been dying to get to the skate rink and have some fun. There's only so much I can do when it's miserably hot outside. Bike rides and ice cream are great but now we're all broke for real so we've had to stay busy inside as temperatures crept up to a sweltering 105 degrees.

Jules and their mom ride with me and my parents to the skate rink, and Aaron and Cedrick meet us there just as we pull up.

Cedrick's dad has his custom skates slung over his shoulder in a bag that has King of the Rink emblazoned on the front in big gold letters. His stepdad, Mr. Alex, has his camera out and ready to go.

"Alex is gonna capture my return to the rink on film," Mr. Ethan says triumphantly.

Mr. Alex and Cedrick exchange glances.

"He hasn't been on these skates since high school," says Mr. Alex. "The only thing I'm about to capture is him shattering his tailbone."

Cedrick laughs but his dad just ignores him. "Just wait," Mr. Ethan says. "I'll show y'all."

The Royal Roller Rink has been around since my parents were kids and it's always packed on the weekends but this fundraiser is for students and staff only so it's not as chaotic as it usually is. Everybody from school is here, including Adrianna and her minions. They already have their stank faces on, but I'm determined to ignore them and have fun. Me and Jules rush inside with Aaron and Cedrick trailing behind us.

"This place looks great!" Jules says.

Mrs. Lambert is helping Mr. Hansen hang a banner across the entryway that says Welcome Students! As we pile in the music is already blasting and the lights are so low I can barely see. The disco ball over the rink is lit up and casts little rainbow squares on the floor. The smell of pizza and popcorn and skate deodorizer wafts through the air.

My mom sticks a twenty-dollar bill in my hand. "Why don't y'all go rent skates and we'll stake out a bench."

I grab Aaron's hand and pull him to the skate rental counter as Jules and Cedrick make bets about who's gonna bust their behind first. All our money is on Cedrick's dad.

We stand in line to get our skates and as we watch more students come in, Adrianna and Leighton walk up and stand directly behind us. I swear I can hear their thoughts rattling around inside their heads. They're gonna make fun of us for being here. They always act like they're too good to participate in stuff like this—fundraisers, bike rodeos, bake sales. They think it's all beneath them. The part that throws me is that they'd make fun of us if we weren't here, too. They'd say our parents wouldn't let us come and then go on and on about how sheltered we all are. There's no winning with people like Adrianna or Leighton.

"I'm surprised they're even here," Adrianna says as she smacks her gum and blows bubbles between sentences. She's talking loud enough for us to hear but not speaking directly to us, which is what my mom calls "passive-aggressive." She says it's annoying and I have to agree.

"Weirdos," Leighton mumbles.

I shake my head and look down at the floor. This is not what I came here for and I have a bad feeling she is going to try and ruin our night.

Aaron's brows bunch together and he narrows his eyes. "Hey, Jules," he says. "Duck."

Jules immediately hunches forward. Aaron shakes up a can of soda he's snagged from somewhere and pops the top right in Adrianna's face, drenching her from head to toe in the bright orange liquid.

"Oh man," Aaron says. "How'd that happen? I'm so sorry. Somebody must've shaken this can up. Hate it when that happens."

Adrianna lets out a yelp, then a gasp. "You did that on purpose!" She steps close to Aaron and puts her finger in his face. "Wait till I tell my dad. You're gonna be sorry."

Aaron takes a step back but Adrianna still manages to knock against his shoulder as she brushes by him and storms off toward the bathroom.

"You really shouldn't have done that," Leighton says.

I see something in Leighton's face that nobody else seems to notice. Leighton isn't being mean, she's saying it like she feels sorry for us. She rushes off after Adrianna without another word.

"That was the best thing I've ever seen!" Cedrick says, snorting and gasping as he laughs himself half to death.

Aaron grins as we all revel in the little bit of payback on Adrianna for her constant bullying before grabbing our skates and lacing up.

"Come on," I say excitedly. "Let's get out on the floor."

Aaron struggles to keep himself upright between me and Jules. A little girl, probably six or seven, skates by us holding on to a rig made of PVC pipe and pool noodles that acts as a support so she doesn't fall.

"I need one of those," Aaron says.

Cedrick zooms by us and does a full spin.

"Show off," I tease. "You give your dad a hard time but he passed his skating skills down to you."

"That's my boy!" Cedrick's dad calls from the rail where our parents are chitchatting and eating pizza. "Get it, Ced!"

Cedrick pretends to be annoyed but he can't hide his cheesy grin.

"I feel like a newborn baby deer," Aaron says, his legs tangled up under him. "I've never done this before."

"You're doing good," Jules tells him. "Try to keep your knees bent. That way if you fall, you'll already be halfway to the ground."

We circle the floor over and over as all our favorite songs play. The DJ, who is actually just Coach Acosta in skinny jeans and a sparkly hat, blasts the "Hokey Pokey" and everybody forms a big circle to follow the instructions of the dance. Cedrick's dad laces up his skates and hits the floor as my dad watches with a pained look on his face. I stop at the rail in front of where my parents are posted up and retie my left skate.

"Roller skating is a tailbone fracture waiting to happen," my dad says.

"That's what I'm sayin'," says Mr. Alex. "I'd never recover."

"Sure you would," says my mom. "Don't be so down on yourself."

They exchange a glance that tells me I'm not in on whatever they're talking about so I mind my business and keep circling the rink.

Cedrick's dad is a little rusty but after a few minutes he's cutting through groups of people and doing spins. Mr. Alex snaps a picture of him every time he goes by.

"We should get some pizza before it's all gone," Cedrick says.

"Good idea," I say. "My stomach is rumbling anyway."

Me and Jules steer Aaron off the rink and onto the carpet where it's a little easier for him to keep his feet from slipping out from under him. I grab a slice of pizza and a Coke and find an empty table. We all pile into the booth. As Cedrick and Jules scarf down their slices and as Aaron chugs his soda I notice Mr. Rupert standing against the wall near the entryway. It's so dark in the shadows off the main rink that I can barely see him, but his bald head is catching the reflection from the disco ball.

"Mr. Rupert is over there," I say. "Lookin' like a whole creep."

Cedrick's head snaps up.

"Don't make it obvious," I say quickly. "If you make eye contact he'll come over here and yell at us for chewing with our mouths open or somethin'."

"Who hurt him?" Aaron asks. "Does he need a hug? What is it?"

We ugly-laugh like a pack of hyenas and Jules has to cover their mouth with a napkin to keep from spitting out their drink.

Cedrick lowers his head. "I didn't think he'd be here. He

seems like he hates fun and kids and this place has a lot of both."

"Yeah," I say. "This doesn't seem like the type of place he'd want to be. He always looks so angry. If kids annoy him so much why is he a school counselor? Did he know what that meant when he signed up?"

Suddenly someone is standing by our booth, blocking our view of Mr. Rupert. It's Mrs. Lambert.

"Having a good time?" she asks as she slides into the booth next to Cedrick.

"We were until we saw Mr. Clean over there," I say.

"Y'all are so wrong for calling him that," she says as she stifles a laugh. "Has he said anything else to any of you?"

"He told me to stop taking the shortcut home," I say. "He said it wasn't safe. And the other day he told me to keep my eyes up—whatever that's supposed to mean."

Mrs. Lambert sucks her teeth. "He seems to take his job very seriously. I think he was a high school counselor before. He's used to dealing with older kids. Maybe just try and steer clear of him until he gets a better feel for how we do things around here." She turns to Aaron. "How are things going? I see the Squad has taken you under their wing. Everybody getting along?"

Aaron nods but keeps his head down, his eyes on the table. "I've never been so happy to be at a new school."

Jules pats his hand and a little knot grows in my throat.

We'd spent almost every day together since he got here and we hadn't gotten deep into what he and his mom were doing before they moved to our street but he did say that they'd moved around a lot. He's hoping this time will be different and that they can stay. I'm hoping for that, too. He's like a piece of a puzzle we didn't even know we were missing. Now that we have it, we can't let it go.

I try to sneak a look over at Mr. Rupert but he's gone now.

"Do your lizards have names?" Jules asks.

"What?" Mrs. Lambert asks. She's staring across the room at the spot where Mr. Rupert had been standing.

"Your lizards," Jules says. "You said you got the roaches for them to eat."

Cedrick drops his slice of pizza onto his plate and crosses his arms over his chest.

"Oh right," Mrs. Lambert says, regaining her focus and turning back to us. "Bert and Ernie. They're a handful." She turns her focus back to the crowd.

"Mrs. Lambert," I say. "Who's in charge of the lighting? It's way too dark in here and I feel like Mr. Rupert is creepin' around in the shadows."

Mrs. Lambert grins. "I'm not sure but let me see what I can do. Enjoy your pizza and make sure you brush your teeth after drinking all this soda."

"My goal is to have six silver teeth by the summer," says Aaron.

"Your parents will be thrilled to hear that their dental bills are about to go up," Mrs. Lambert says. "At least try to drink some water or something." She pats Aaron on the shoulder and gets up.

My gaze trails her as she zigzags through the crowd and stops to speak to Mr. Rupert, who had reappeared by the skate rental counter. I can't hear them through the din and I can barely see his face due to the combination of dancing lights and shifting shadows but he looks annoyed. He angrily motions to the front entrance and Mrs. Lambert steps toward him. She's not the type of teacher to put up with anybody's attitude and Mr. Rupert steps back, looking stunned.

I nudge Aaron in the ribs. "Look. Mrs. Lambert is probably telling Mr. Rupert to stop walking around here lookin' like a whole demon."

Aaron cranes his neck to look at Mr. Rupert but we both look away quickly as he shifts his gaze to us.

"This dude is gonna make us hate him," says Cedrick, finishing up his pizza. "And he's wearing a sweater. Again."

"He likes sweaters, Ced," Jules says. "Let him live."

I finish my pizza and Jules hands me their pizza crust, which I happily finish for them.

It's almost eight thirty when Mrs. Lambert hoists herself onto a tabletop and asks everyone for their attention.

"We have surpassed our fundraising goal by two hundred dollars," she says excitedly. "Combined with our other fundraising efforts throughout the summer and first part of the school year, I'm happy to say that our library and technology lab will be getting all new equipment and the library will have an extra one thousand dollars to update our shelves!"

The crowd erupts into cheers and thunderous applause. I look for Miss Polk, our librarian, in the crowd. When I see her she's clapping her hands and jumping up and down.

"She's so happy," Jules says, smiling.

"She said we could order all the Miles Morales comics," Cedrick said. "She said I could help her unpack them and put the plastic covers on."

Cedrick and Miss Polk are comic book stans. Ced's been Spider-Man every Halloween since we were little and now that there's one that looks just like him, he can't get enough. He's got posters and T-shirts and even a copy of *Miles Morales: Spider-Man* signed by Jason Reynolds. He keeps it in a lockbox under his bed and guards it like a dragon guards its treasure. Cedrick and Miss Polk even got together to write a letter to the principal when the read-a-thon committee refused to count comics and graphic novels. They actually convinced Ms. Mason to allow them and they've been thick as thieves ever since. They spot each other across the crowd and Cedrick shoots her a big toothy grin and she pumps her fist in the air, her eyes glassy with tears.

In this moment, with everybody smiling and celebrating, it feels like a win but all of that fades as I turn to my parents. My mom is gesturing toward the front doors and Dad is nodding in agreement at whatever she's saying.

"I'm gonna use the bathroom," Aaron says.

I nod and he heads toward the restroom as Mrs. Lambert climbs down and starts shaking hands with the parents and other teachers as the night draws to a close.

I lean close to Jules's ear and lower my voice. "Something's goin' on with my parents."

Jules looks over at them, thinks for a minute, then turns to me. "I think it's the time. This thing is gonna go on longer than it was supposed to."

Outside, the sun is setting. Of course my parents are getting restless. We don't really stay out too late most of the time and with the way they were acting the night of the BBQ, it makes me wonder what's going on with them. Me and Jules plop down and start taking off our skates.

Cedrick takes off his skate and sniffs the inside. He rears back. "I don't think that spray they put in the skates is gonna be able to handle this kind of funk." He scoots the skates away from him. "They might have to burn those."

Cedrick's dad comes over and collects our skates and takes them back to the counter.

"Ready to go?" my mom asks.

Miss Kim checks her phone, then looks around.

"He went to the bathroom," I say, figuring she's looking for Aaron.

"Oh, okay," she says, glancing at her phone, then toward the bathroom.

"We're gonna head out," Cedrick's dad says. He gives us all a big hug and Cedrick races his stepdad to their car.

My mom puts her arm around my shoulder as the crowd files out. We wait right outside the front doors so that we can snag Aaron when he's done in the restroom.

"Y'all don't have to wait around," says Miss Kim.

"You sure?" my dad asks. "We don't mind."

Me and Jules laugh as Cedrick and his parents drive by. Cedrick presses his face against the back window and his nose scrunches up as his breath fogs the glass.

"So ugly," I call out.

His dad gives us a wave and they turn out of the parking lot.

"Y'all go ahead," says Aaron's mom. "That boy is about as lactose intolerant as they come. He's probably tearing that bathroom up." She pauses. "Don't tell him I told you."

"Miss Kim," I say. "I can't hold on to that kind of information and not use it against him."

"Boog is the last person who should hold something like that over somebody's head," my mom says. "She isn't allowed in my bathroom at all. Might make the wallpaper peel right off."

"Mom!" I say, the heat of embarrassment rising in my face.

Mom and Miss Kim laugh together, leaning on each other like they can't stand up. Listen. It's not my fault that tacos are my weakness and that my colon can't handle it. It's just the way things are but am I gonna stop eating breakfast tacos with extra cheese and hot sauce? Absolutely not.

We say bye to her and me and Jules scramble into the backseat of my dad's SUV.

Jules lowers their voice and puts their mouth close to my ear. "It's so late. It's, like, nine thirty."

"I know," I whisper. We're usually in bed at this time or at least in the house. My heart is beating fast and there's a nervous flutter in my stomach, like we're doing something we shouldn't be but as I glance outside, nobody else seems to be nervous. Nobody else is in a rush. People are talking outside their cars, kids are messing around in the parking lot. It's all so . . . normal.

A horn blares outside. There's a loud crunch.

"Gotta be kidding me," my dad says. "Somebody just hit Principal Mason's car."

Me and Jules press our faces against the glass to get a better look. Ms. Mason is standing outside her car with an irritated look on her face as one of the other parents examines the damage.

"People don't know how to drive," I say.

"When did you get your license?" my mom asks, smiling. "Since you're an expert."

"I know I'm gonna be a better driver than this fool," I say, looking at the scene. The other parent had hit Ms. Mason's car while it was parked. "How did he even do that?"

Minutes tick by as other cars file into the line heading

toward the exit. Brake lights drench the inside of our van in a hazy red glow. I glance out the back window and catch a glimpse of Mr. Rupert. He has his hands stuffed in his pockets, his head down. He's speed-walking away from the entrance to the rink. Nobody else is around except Aaron's mom, who stands alone by the front door. Her expression is different now. Her mouth is drawn tight, her eyes narrow. She looks worried.

CHAPTER 7

The worst thing about Monday mornings is my mom. Monday feels like the end of the best part of the week—the weekend. But my mom is an optimist. She looks at Mondays like a chance to start over, to do something bigger and better than you did the week before. All I want to do on Monday mornings is sleep in. I hit snooze on my alarm twice before my mom comes in and cuts the light on.

"Rise and shine," she says in a singsong voice.

I cover my eyes and bury my face in my pillow. "Can I just stay home?"

"You got a fever?" she asks.

"Maybe," I say, knowing good and well I don't.

"Throwing up? Diarrhea?"

"That's nasty," I say as I sit up and pull my bonnet off my head.

"You're in perfect health, so, no, you're not staying home," she says. She gently pulls the covers off me and I yank them back up.

"Please, Mom," I say, knowing she's not gonna change her mind but still giving her my best please-feel-sorry-for-me face. "I'm so tired."

She puts her hand down on her hip. "I don't know why your school thought it'd be a good idea to have a fundraiser on a Sunday night." She shakes her head. "Up, Boog. Right now."

I drag myself out of bed, brush my teeth, get dressed, and meet my dad in the kitchen. He hands me two waffles with peanut butter and sliced bananas sandwiched in between.

"Breakfast of champions," he says.

My mom comes in and kisses him, then me, and leaves for work.

"I'll be here till Mom gets off, then I have to work a late shift," he says. "You'll help out later?"

I nod as I stuff my mouth with peanut-butter-covered waffles. I take out my phone and send a message to the group chat.

JULES: I'm so tired!!!!

CEDRICK: No more Sunday night parties.

ME: We're such babies. We were only up till like 10

CEDRICK: Well I guess I'm a baby then because I'm ready to go right back to sleep.

ME: Aaron . . . you still sleep?

He doesn't answer and I wonder if he's lucky enough to

have a parent who lets him stay home for no reason other than he's extra tired every once in a while.

I grab my backpack and go out to meet Jules in the front drive. My dad waves from the porch as Cedrick comes to meet us and we all hop on our bikes and ride to the corner to wait for Arron but as we pedal up, his mom's car isn't in the driveway.

"Maybe his mom drove him to school," Jules says. "Lucky."

I take out my phone and send another text to Aaron.

ME: Are you home? We're out here.

We hang around for a few minutes but he doesn't respond. As I look up at his house I don't see any lights on.

"We gotta go or we're gonna be late," Cedrick says. "His mom probably took him. We can't be late because we have to do our multiplication quiz and if I get a hundred percent, my dad says I never have to eat vegan meat ever again."

Jules huffs. "There's no way it can be that bad."

Cedrick stares them dead in the eye. "It is."

I glance up at the house again. I hope Aaron isn't mad at us for leaving the rink before he was done in the bathroom.

"Let's go," I say. "We'll catch up with him at school."

When we pull up to the bike rack, there are three police cars in the parking lot and two more on the street. I take a deep breath. This isn't a lockdown. Those always scare me a little, even when it's just a drill. But the police don't have their lights on, no one is running or scared. It's not like something is happening right now. Students are going in and out like usual but everyone is quieter than normal.

"What is going on here?" I ask. I lock up my bike and walk inside with Jules and Cedrick at my side. "What's with the police?"

"Maybe they finally caught on to Mr. Rupert," Cedrick says. "I bet you they found out he's a serial killer or something."

"Don't say that," says Jules. "This looks serious."

Kids are huddled up, whispering to one another. They stare at us as we walk up the front steps and go inside. In the halls, the scene is even stranger. Teachers are on their phones in plain view. The same teachers who act like you've committed the most heinous crime imaginable if your phone rings during class. I catch little pieces of people's conversations as we make our way to class.

"What did the police say?" one girl asks.

"They asked me if I knew him," says her friend. "I didn't. Now my mom's worried."

A creeping dread settles at the base of my neck and then begins to seep into my bones. I'm not exactly sure why. All I know is that the air feels heavy, like it's too hot to breathe. I pull at the neck of my T-shirt as I walk into Mrs. Lambert's homeroom and sit down. Mrs. Lambert isn't here yet.

Jules slides into the seat next to me. "Why is everybody acting so weird?"

Cedrick sits down behind us and leans forward. "Where's Aaron?"

"Isn't he your friend?" Adrianna pipes up from her seat in the back of the class. "And you don't know?"

"Know what?" I ask.

Adrianna rolls her eyes and snickers behind her hands. I have to turn away from her before I get too worked up. She always manages to flip stuff back around on me. It doesn't work in Mrs. Lambert's class but I've gotten in way more trouble for talking back to her than she's ever gotten in for harassing me every other day.

Mrs. Lambert sweeps into the room with Ms. Mason. Behind them is a police officer. A hush falls over the class as everyone turns to look at them.

"Class," Mrs. Lambert says, her tone deadly serious. "I need you all to remain in your seats." She looks right at me. The whites of her eyes are red. Like she's been crying. "Malika, I need you to go with Ms. Mason for just a moment."

I exchange glances with Jules. The other students all watch me as I get up and follow Ms. Mason out of the classroom.

"What's going on?" I ask. It still feels like there's a rock in the pit of my stomach. Something's off. No. Not just off . . . something is very, very wrong.

Ms. Mason gently rests her hand on my shoulder. "Your parents are in the office. We'll talk in there."

My parents? I'm more confused and the rock in my stomach suddenly feels like a boulder.

I follow Ms. Mason down the hall, which is completely empty. Even during class there are usually a few students and teachers wandering around. Now, there's no one. Not a single person and the classroom doors are all closed.

Ms. Mason leads me into her private office where my mom and dad are sitting, whispering to each other. The police officer follows us in and closes the door. Mom pulls me down next to her.

My palms are sweaty and my heart is racing a mile a minute. "What's happening? Are you guys okay?"

My mom nods but she doesn't speak. My dad looks down at the floor, opens his mouth to say something but then stops.

I start to shake, like I've been out in the cold without a coat for too long. "Somebody please tell me what's going on."

Ms. Mason sits at her desk and folds her hands. "Malika, Officer Morgan here would like to ask you and your family some questions, but we want to be very clear that no one is in trouble and that what's going on may be hard to understand, maybe even a little scary. But we're all here for you. Okay, sweetie?"

I just nod. Ms. Mason has never called me sweetie. Ever.

Mom takes my hand in hers and squeezes it tight. I stare down at the scars crisscrossing her knuckles.

"Baby, Aaron never made it home after the fundraiser at the skating rink. He—he's missing."

I raise my head and look at her. The expression on her face scares me. Her chin wobbles, her eyes are wet. It's like she's trying desperately not to cry. I look back and forth between my parents and Ms. Mason and then to Officer Morgan.

"This isn't funny," I say.

"I wish it were a joke," says Officer Morgan. "A prank. At this point I wouldn't even be upset but that doesn't appear to be the case." He straightens up and takes out a small notepad and a pen. "Aaron is new to the school but you two were friends, is that right?"

"Why are you saying it like that?" I ask. "We *are* friends. And what do you mean he's missing? He was at the rink with us last night."

"His mother was waiting for him to come out of the skating venue but he never did," says Officer Morgan.

This doesn't make sense. I can't fully understand what the officer is saying to me. An image of Miss Kim's face pops up in my head and I can't get past how worried she looked as we pulled out of the parking lot. We were gonna wait but she told us we should go. We should have waited.

My dad reaches over and puts his hand on my knee, weighing it down because it's started to shake uncontrollably just like the rest of me. "Malika, I need you to tell the officer everything you can remember about last night in as much detail as possible. Can you do that?"

I try to make my heart slow down but I can't. I stumble over my words as I tell the officer everything about the night before. We'd all met up at the rink, ate pizza, skated, joked around. A knot hardens in my throat and my hands get all sweaty. I rub them on my jeans.

"This can't be happening," I say.

Mom pulls me close to her. My dad tells Officer Morgan about the fender bender in the parking lot and how we'd offered to stay and wait with Aaron's mom but that we had to get home because the fundraiser had run late.

"We should have waited for him to come out," I say. A sob breaks from my chest and tears sting my eyes. "We should've gone in to make sure he was okay."

"Boog, this isn't your fault," my dad says. He's about to cry, too. "Officer Morgan, are there any leads? Anything at all? What can we do to help?"

"We're questioning everyone who was at the function," says Officer Morgan. "We're reviewing security footage and we're trying to see if there was anyone there who shouldn't have been. It's my understanding that it was a closed event."

Ms. Mason nods.

"Have you talked to Mr. Rupert?" I ask.

Officer Morgan narrows his eyes at me. "Not yet. Is there a specific reason I should?"

"He was there," I say. "He was walking away from the rink. Like, speed-walking away. I saw him."

My mom and dad look at each other.

"And he's been creeping around me and my friends," I say.

"Boog—" my mom starts.

"Mom, he's weird. And he's been telling me I need to be careful like he knows me or something."

Officer Morgan scribbles a few notes in his notepad.

"Mr. Rupert is new to our campus," Ms. Mason says. "Everyone is still getting used to him. He's an awkward sort of man but I think that's just his way. He has a laundry list of degrees and more references than I can count."

"So he went to college and he has friends," I say angrily. "That doesn't mean he can't be a creep."

"Miss Wilson, please," Ms. Mason says. "Please try to calm down."

"I—I don't want to calm down. Something happened to Aaron. We have to find him."

Officer Morgan pats me on the shoulder. "I'm sure he'll turn up."

I shake my head, about to protest when my dad stands up. "I think you should come home with us, Boog."

"There's really no need," Officer Morgan says, smiling at me. "You're safe at school."

"Even still," my dad says. "I think it's best if we bring her home. Aaron is her friend. This is hard for her to hear."

Ms. Mason sits back in her chair. "Mr. Wilson, I understand you're a bit—overprotective."

"Overprotective?" Officer Morgan asks. "Can't really blame a man for wanting to protect his child."

"From vampires?" Ms. Mason says it so low it's almost like a whisper.

Officer Morgan laughs but when my dad doesn't, he quiets

himself. "Mr. Wilson, you can't seriously be concerned about vamps."

My dad shakes his head. "I don't have to explain myself to you but I believe in being cautious."

"But the Reaping—" Officer Morgan begins but my dad cuts him off.

"I know what happened at the Reaping," my dad snaps. He glares at the officer as he speaks. "That doesn't change a lifetime of looking over my shoulder and keeping myself prepared for anything. And now my daughter's friend is missing. Excuse me, but I'll continue to do what I need to do to keep myself and my family safe."

"Bet you still use vampire repellent," Officer Morgan says in a tone that tells me he thinks it's dumb.

My dad's face is all twisted up. His wide eyes are locked on Officer Morgan and his hand is clenched at his side.

"Are we done here?" my mom asks, setting her hand gently on my dad's arm.

Ms. Mason nods.

"C'mon, Boog," my dad says, pulling me toward the door.

"What? No. Dad, I don't need to leave, I just—I need to talk to Cedrick and Jules." This doesn't feel real. Aaron is missing? We were just together, laughing and eating pizza. This can't be happening.

My mom slips her arm around my shoulder and guides me out of the office with my dad following close behind. The ride home is a blur. I try to text Jules and Cedrick but neither of them answers. I text Aaron.

ME: Where are you??? Please come home.

I know it won't make a difference but I have to do something, anything. Before I know it, we're inside my house and I'm sitting on the couch in a daze. My mom sits beside me but my dad stands in the front room, looking out the window, his mouth drawn tight.

"Boog, I know this is a lot to take in," says my mom. "We're gonna do everything we can to find him. I promise."

"He's just gone?" I ask. It's not the right question but it's all I can think of. "How? How can he just be gone? We—we were there. Me and Jules and Ced and—and—" I can't even say his name before I break down in tears again.

My dad shakes his head. "There are things in this world that I will never understand—"

"But you don't have to be afraid," my mom cuts in. "We'll find him and get him home."

She and my dad look at each other in a way that scares me. They are afraid but trying really hard not to show it.

"I'm gonna go to my room." I need to be alone for a minute so I can think.

"Sure," my mom says. "Take all the time you need, baby."

I go up to my room and close the door. I immediately take out my phone and call Jules. They pick up on the first ring.

"Hey," they say.

"You home, too?" I ask.

"Yeah. My mom came and got me. Boog, what is goin' on? Aaron is missing?"

I slump down onto my bed. "I don't understand. We saw him go into the bathroom, right?"

"Yeah, but he didn't come back out."

I picture his mom's face in my mind. "Can you come over?"

"I can't," they say. "My mom says we need to talk about this and she doesn't want me going anywhere. You talked to Cedrick yet?"

"No," I say.

"I saw his dad going into the school when we were leaving," Jules says. "But their car isn't in the driveway and he didn't answer my text."

I lie across my bed and stare up at the ceiling. "So what do we do now?"

"I don't even know," Jules says quietly. "I just don't know. What can we do?" There's a long pause. "I'll call you later okay?"

"Okay." We hang up. I'm so confused and not just that. I'm angry, I'm worried to death about Aaron. Is he out there somewhere? Is he hurt? Did someone take him? Nobody saw what happened to him? Nobody heard anything? I have too many questions and not enough answers. It just doesn't make sense.

CHAPTER 8

We search for Aaron for a whole week. My parents take turns going out during the afternoons, walking shoulder to shoulder with other people from the neighborhood. Down the entire length of the Green and back up it. I don't even want to think about what it means if they find something, so when they come back with nothing, I'm relieved and then angry and sad all over again

Flyers with Aaron's smiling face go up on every electrical pole, every grocery store bulletin board, every social media site. The police talk to everybody who was at the rink that night but don't learn anything new.

Every day my mom and Cedrick's dad take turns driving me and Jules and Cedrick to school. And it's the only time in the past week we got to spend together. None of us are allowed out. My mom and dad make it clear that they will be waiting outside as soon as the bell rings. No biking to and from school anymore and once I'm home, I stay there.

And there's something else, something that scares me more than just about anything. Usually my parents make sure everything is locked up at night. That's a normal thing to do, but now, every single night they systematically check each door, making sure they're locked by pulling roughly on the handles. After they secure the doors, they split up—Mom goes upstairs and Dad goes to the basement. They check each window. They test each window lock. They pull the curtains closed and test the porch lights, which are now equipped with bulbs that shine as bright as a floodlight, only they have a strange blue-purple tint to them.

When I'm at school it doesn't seem like anybody else's parents are keeping them locked up at home. Yeah, there are more car rides than normal, fewer bikes in the bike rack, but my parents along with Jules's and Ced's families are more protective than they've ever been.

The following Sunday I spend the afternoon in a group chat with Jules and Cedrick. It's the closest thing we've got to hanging out.

CEDRICK: I can't take it no more I GOTTA GET OUT OF HERE

JULES: 'Lita has been letting me do whatever I want as long as I'm in the house. If I put one toe by the door she's on me like a fly on poop.

ME: Gross but accurate. I watched every rerun of
That's So Raven, Black Panther for the millionth time
(RIP Chadwick), and I read three books

CEDRICK: I want to help look for Aaron. Why are our
parents acting like somebody is out there trying to get us?

I think about what he's saying and he's right. My parents
have been protective to the extreme. Not just regular overprotective either—sleeping in shifts, making rounds through the
house every hour all through the night. They think I don't
hear them creeping around. Aaron is our friend and it's just too
close for them not to be worried about the rest of us but this is
something else.

After Cedrick tries to devise a plan to get a pizza ordered
and after Jules offers to send over some protein bars, to which
Cedrick sends a GIF of a guy puking his guts out, we end our
chat and agree to meet up the next day at school.

Later that night, my dad cooks and my mom has the night
off so we watch TV in the living room. The signal gets choppy
as a light rain patters on the roof.

"It's late anyway," my dad says, switching off the TV
just as the signal goes out completely. "Time for bed."

Everything feels sticky and damp even with the AC on.
The tapping of rain starts low, then climbs until it's like white
noise blocking out just about every other sound except my
racing thoughts. It can't drown those out and all I can think
of is Aaron.

"You'll still go searching for him, even if it rains tomorrow?" I ask. I swallow the lump in my throat. "Promise you'll still go?"

My mom's eyes mist over and she glances toward the front window. My dad stands and puts his arms around me. "I promise. Rain or shine, we'll be out there. We won't stop till he's home." He kisses me on the top of my head. "Try to get some rest."

"Night, Boog," my mom says, her voice thick with sadness.

My dad watches me go up the stairs. I open my bedroom door but I don't go in. I stand at the top of the stairs in the darkened hallway. My parents have been having conversations when they think I'm not listening. I only catch bits and pieces because they always wait until they think I'm asleep or not paying attention. They are keeping something from me and I think it has to do with Aaron. So, I wait—barely breathing, not daring to move.

"Tre," my mom says in a whisper that I have to strain to hear above the rainfall. "We have to do something."

"We *are* doing something," Dad says. "We're out there every day looking for him."

"That's not what I mean and you know it," says Mom. "We have to do *more*."

"Belinda said she hasn't seen anything out of the ordinary," my dad says.

"Belinda from the morgue? You checked in with her?"

"I felt like I had to," Dad says. "I know it's not smart. It could cause a ripple effect but I had to do something."

My chest feels like it's gonna cave in. The morgue? Why would my parents be talking to somebody there, unless—no. I bite my lip to keep it from quivering. I angrily wipe the tears that sting my eyes. Aaron's not dead. We're gonna find him. We have to. I shift my weight, leaning closer to the top of the stairs. A bolt of lightning splits the air outside and lights up the hallway for a brief second before a clap of thunder rumbles through the night sky.

"Nothing abnormal—yet," says my dad. "And I don't want to assume anything."

"Me either," says my mom. "But I have this feeling, in my gut. Something I haven't felt since before Boog was born. Since before the—"

A gust of wind rattles the house and I lose the last little bit of what my mom is saying as they move toward the kitchen. There's no sense trying to tiptoe down there to eavesdrop. There are too many creaky boards in the floor. I slink back down the hall and crawl into bed, pulling the covers up to my neck.

None of this feels real. How can Aaron just be gone without a trace? Every day I wake up and for one second I think about Jules and Cedrick and Aaron. I start to think of what we'll do and if we'll get to plan a sleepover soon so we can order pizza and watch movies and take pictures with my new camera lens. It's like everything is normal for one quick moment and then it all crashes down on me again. Aaron is missing. Aaron is gone.

Tap . . . tap

The rain is pelting my window so hard it almost sounds like it does when it starts to hail.

Tap . . . tap

Another flash of lightning rips through the sky and even through closed curtains it lights up my room. The rumble of thunder sounds farther away now and after a few minutes the rain slows to a light drizzle. It makes me sleepy enough to close my eyes, pushing all the bad thoughts away. At least for a little while.

Tap . . . tap

I open my eyes. I listen. The rain has stopped.

Tap . . . tap

I glance at my window. The curtain is completely closed.

Tap . . . tap

I roll out of bed and tiptoe to the middle of my room where I stand as still as I possibly can.

The noise is coming from outside.

I take a step toward the window but I stop. My stomach drops and I suddenly feel like I shouldn't move or breathe. It's the same feeling I get when I tip off the top of the Goliath roller coaster at Six Flags. The little hairs on the back of my neck and arms stand straight up. I'm scared to death but I can't figure out exactly why. The storm? No. I've been listening to those sounds since forever. The dark? I'm not scared of the dark. I don't even sleep with a light on. So, what is it?

The tapping stops and I jump back into bed and pull the covers over my head.

CHAPTER 9

During the night, the storm picked back up and the wind knocked down a tree in our yard. It broke our fence and I think it might've broken my dad's brain, too. He's standing in the yard when I come down for breakfast and I can hear him yelling . . . at the tree.

"What is going on here?" he hollers. "My fence is ruined! Why would you do this?"

I look at my mom. "Is Dad gonna be okay?"

My mom sighs and pushes a plate of cut-up pancakes toward me. "Define 'okay.'"

"Yikes," I say as I shovel the sticky sweet squares into my mouth. "Is he still driving us to school?"

"Celia is going to take you today," she says as my dad lets out a loud grunt from somewhere outside. "He'll take y'all tomorrow."

"Or we could just ride our bikes like we always do," I say.

My mom sets down her cup of coffee a little too hard. "No. And please don't bring it up again because I'm not budging on this."

I finish my pancakes and put my plate in the sink. "Are things ever gonna go back to the way they were before?"

My mom and I stand there just staring at each other.

"I want it to, baby," she says. "But if I tell you yes, I'd be lying. The truth is I don't know." She walks to the front door. "Jules is waiting in the car. Better hurry up so you don't keep Celia waiting."

I grab my backpack and Mom walks me to the curb. Dad waves to me but his face is all sweaty and I can see that he's in a bad mood. One of the big trees in our yard lies on its side, its branches charred to a crisp. Lightning must've struck it directly. On the way down, it took out a car-sized piece of our fence.

"This is the perfect time to do some upgrades," Mom says as she walks me out to the car.

My dad nods at her and takes out his phone.

Jules leans across the back seat of Miss Celia's car and pushes the door open. I slip in beside them as our moms chit-chat about how reckless I'm being by asking to ride my bike.

"Boog, look," Jules says. They look down at their phone and tap the screen, then gesture to their mom.

"Right," I say.

We move our conversation to text.

JULES: 'Lita was talking to my mom last night and she said this is dangerous.

My skin pricks up.

ME: What's dangerous?

JULES: I don't know. I caught them midconversation and then they just changed the subject like I wouldn't notice.

ME: Sounds like my parents. I don't know what's going on but I don't like it.

JULES: We'll talk when we get to school

I glance up and realize it's a little too quiet. Mom and Miss Celia have stopped talking.

I slip my phone back in my bag as my mom walks up the driveway and we pull off.

I wait for Cedrick in Mrs. Lambert's homeroom and when he doesn't show up after two whole minutes, I start to panic. My hands get all sweaty and my heart beats so hard and fast I can feel it pounding in my head. When he finally walks in, I bum-rush him and hug him tight. He hugs me back and I hear Adrianna snicker but I don't care. She's just mad none of her friends like her enough to miss her when she's not here.

"Listen," Cedrick says as we sit down. "Have your parents been acting weird? Like, weirder than normal?"

Me and Jules nod.

"See?" I say quietly, keeping my voice low. "Something is up."

"My dad came into my room at least five times last night," Cedrick says. "Talkin' 'bout he's checking the locks on my window because of that storm." He frowns. "He has the worst I'm-lying face you've ever seen."

"Why would he lie to you about checking the locks?" Jules asks.

"He's never done that before," Cedrick says. "Not for a storm. You know how many storms be rollin' in outta nowhere. And how is the storm gonna open my window? If anything the glass would just break, right? My dads never worried about locking everything up like this. Ever."

I think about the tapping at my window and the unsettling feeling of being deathly afraid washes over me again. "I over-heard my parents talking about somebody named Belinda who works at the morgue."

"Excuse me?" Jules tilts their head to the side and stares at me. "Why are they talking to somebody at a morgue?"

I shrug. "That's what I'm saying. And my dad told my mom that Belinda, whoever she is, said she hadn't seen anything *abnormal*."

"Abnormal how?" Cedrick asks.

Jules shakes their head. "I don't get it but the way 'Lita was talking was definitely weird. Why are they acting like this? Is it what's going on with Aaron?"

"That's part of it," I say. "But there's gotta be more to it than that."

"They're worried about your safety," says Mr. Rupert, who snuck up on us and is standing at the edge of my desk.

I glance up at him and have to use every ounce of strength I have to keep my jaw from falling open. He looks like he hasn't slept. Ever. The bags under his eyes are so dark I wonder if maybe somebody beat him up. He looks rough.

He leans down, pressing his hands into the top of my desk. "A young man has gone missing and your parents, along with the parents of every other student in this school, are worried sick about him and about you." Mr. Rupert sounds genuinely irritated. "Maybe try showing a little understanding."

"We are," I say. Now I'm a little defensive. Why is he all in our conversation? "We know our parents are worried. We're worried, too."

"Please try to remember that your parents were alive when the last of the vampires were wiped out. They surely remember what it was like to live in a world where people disappeared a little too often. I know I do."

For the very first time since I'd met him, Mr. Rupert seems like he might be more than just a nosy old man. He looks sad as he talks about living under the threat of vampires.

"It's not like that anymore, though," I remind him.

"You're right," he says. "It's not. But that doesn't mean your parents don't remember how it felt. Cut them a little slack until your friend is found."

"Until he's found *safe*," I say. I am not going to let Mr. Rupert or anybody else get it in their head that Aaron isn't coming home safe and sound.

Mr. Rupert gives me a little nod but he doesn't correct what he said. I go right back to thinking he's just a bitter old man who likes to be in everybody's business.

"Why does your coat have leather patches on the elbows?" Cedrick asks, a little crooked smile on his lips. "Are you afraid something is gonna happen—to your elbows?"

Leave it to Cedrick to jump right to the jokes. Mr. Rupert opens his mouth like he's going to say something. He looks like he wants to tell Cedrick to shut up and I try to think of how fast his dad would get here to fight Mr. Rupert. Cedrick's dads don't play when it comes to him, which is probably why he's quick to back talk.

Mrs. Lambert walks in right as Mr. Rupert is pressing his lips together so hard his chin wrinkles up.

"Morning, class," she says. She's clutching a cup of coffee that is probably gonna be sitting cold on her desk at the end of the day. She always gets so wrapped up with our class work that she never gets a chance to drink it. "I know you all have had some difficult days but—" She stops short when she sees Mr. Rupert. "Everything all right?"

"Just encouraging your students to be a little more understanding of the current situation," he says, straightening out his jacket.

Mrs. Lambert sets her hand on her hip and tilts her head. "Well, are you done encouraging them? I have a class to teach."

Mr. Rupert marches out of the room without so much as a

nod in Mrs. Lambert's direction and I know she'll take that personally. She huffs loudly, mumbling something under her breath, then begins her lesson.

"Mr. Keller is out sick today and he asked me to help y'all review for your upcoming history quiz," she says. "So let's go over the basics. For anyone feeling a little uneasy about this topic, please keep in mind that in the twenty years since the Reaping, there have been no credible reports of vampire sightings or bites. There have been no reports of anyone being turned."

Mrs. Lambert's words should be comforting, but I'm not going to feel better until Aaron is back safe and sound.

"Who can tell me why vampires were so low in number at the time of the Reaping?" asks Mrs. Lambert.

Adrianna raises her hand and Mrs. Lambert calls on her.

"Because most people who were bitten by a vamp died," she says.

Mrs. Lambert nods. "Correct. The statistics show that ninety-five percent of the time, a vampire bite resulted in death. Now, was it also possible to be bitten and survive?"

I raise my hand and she nods at me.

"Yes," I say. "You could get bitten and survive and still not become a vamp yourself. It was uncommon but it has happened."

Mrs. Lambert bristled. "Can you imagine?" She shook her head and continued. "And what was the rarest occurrence of all?"

It was Cedrick's turn to answer. "The making of another vampire."

Mrs. Lambert smiled. "Correct. Turning a human being into a vampire was the most uncommon occurrence after an interaction with the undead. Making a vampire required the human victim to have an AB negative blood type, the most unique blood type there is. This quirk made their ability to increase their numbers almost impossible."

"That's why the Vanquishers wiped them out," Adrianna says as the class claps and hollers. "Wiped them right off the map!"

As much as I despise Adrianna, she's right.

Mrs. Lambert waits for everyone to calm down before proceeding. "They were actual monsters," she says, her tone deadly serious. "They were creatures of the night. They could turn themselves into shadows or swarms of rats. They were feared above all else and although they've been eradicated there is still fear. That was another lesser known facet of their power—the ability to live on in the memory of the human population, to inspire fear even all these years later." Mrs. Lambert takes a swig of her coffee. "Pen and paper out, please. Let's do a little vocabulary review."

As we all take out our supplies I can't shake the uneasy feeling that had settled over me from the night before. I struggle to focus on the assignment and just try to keep my head down and look like I'm busy. When the bell rings I gather my things and follow Jules and Cedrick out into the hall.

"You okay, Boog?" Jules asks. "I mean I know you're not. None of us are really."

I shrug. "I don't know. I'll see you at lunch."

I head off to gym, thinking of Aaron, of the strange feeling that won't leave me, of the things my parents have been whispering about. I don't let myself think about what it could mean. If they know something about Aaron, something terrible, they'll tell me. They wouldn't keep that from me.

That afternoon, Miss Celia drops me off at home and Dad is waiting on the porch. He's on his phone as I walk up.

"Just make sure it's the real deal," he says into the phone. "Three nines fine. Can't be anything else and I need it today. Tomorrow at the latest. I gotta get this thing fixed." He hangs up and gives me a big hug before steering me inside.

"What the heck is three nines fine?" I ask. It sounds like something you'd order at a fancy restaurant.

"Some building material for the fence," he says. "How was school?"

"It was okay. Is Mom here?"

"No but she should be home—" His phone buzzes in his hand. He answers it right away. "Were your ears burning?" It must be my mom but my dad's smile fades away almost instantly. "I thought you were coming home early." He gestures to the kitchen where a plastic container sits on the counter.

Takeout. He turns away from me and lowers his voice. "I know you're careful but I just—I didn't want you to have to drive home so late."

I try to listen in but he moves to the living room and the smell of hot egg rolls and chicken fried rice keeps me glued to the kitchen. He finishes up on the phone and comes back to join me.

"Mom's working late. Just you and me and this Chinese food. Think we can handle that?"

I'm already scooping my serving and the serving meant for my mom onto a plate. "Don't even worry about it. Since Mom's not eating, I'll just go ahead and take this."

We eat and I finish my homework in the living room as my dad watches some show about ancient aliens on the TV.

"They don't give humans enough credit," he grumbles as some man who looks like he stuck his finger in an electrical outlet talks about the Great Pyramid.

I want to ask him about what I heard him and my mom talking about the other day but I'm not sure how to bring it up.

"Dad," I say quietly.

"Yeah, Boogie," he says, his eyes still on the TV screen.

"I know I'm supposed to stay out of grown folks' business but—"

"Boog, you've never been real good about that," he chuckles. "I don't know how much I believe in grown folks' business anymore."

"What do you mean?"

"Just that if it's something that affects you, maybe it's not just grown folks' business."

I think for moment. This definitely affects me so I guess it can't hurt to ask.

"I'm sorry, but I heard you talking to Mom about somebody named Belinda at the morgue."

My dad's gaze slowly moves toward me and he mutes the TV.

"You would tell me, right?" I ask. Tears well up in my eyes and I bite down hard to try and keep them from spilling over. "If it was something about Aaron."

Dad pulls me over next to him where I ball up and he puts his arms around me.

"I'm so sorry, Boog," he says. "I didn't mean for you to hear any of that. I just—I don't know. I shouldn't have called her and I shouldn't have let you catch me talking about it."

"You think he's dead?" I ask.

My dad reaches down and turns my face to his. "No. I still have hope that we'll find him and bring him home." I can tell he means it but the way he sighs and looks at the floor makes me wonder what he's not saying. "But I think I owe you a little bit of an explanation."

I wait for him to go on but he hesitates.

"You know what happened to Grandpa," he says.

I don't know what I was expecting him to say but it wasn't

anything that had to do with Grandpa Leo. He died when Dad was little, way before I was even born.

"I was younger than you when he died," my dad says. "I've been thinking about him a lot lately."

"Because of Aaron?" I ask.

"In a way. Yes." He sighs and readjusts his arms around me. "I think about what he would have done if that were me out there." I can feel his heart kick up. His chest rises and falls in big slow waves. "On top of all that, I remember that feeling of losing him. It lives in me." He gently touches his chest. "I fear a loss like that more than anything. So I see your friend go missing, I see the pain in his mother's face. It has been so hard, Boog. Me and your mom have been trying to keep up a front because we don't want you to worry but there are about a million things running through my mind. I'm sorry if you've been worried."

I hug him tight and we sit in the quiet for a long time before he kisses me on the top of the head. "Bedtime, Boogie."

"I love you, Dad," I say.

"I love you, too."

As I make my way upstairs I can hear him locking up. He'll have to go through this new routine of checking every lock, every window, securing every curtain on his own tonight.

In my room, I put on my pajamas and crawl into bed but I lie awake, looking at the ceiling for a long time.

"Aaron, where are you?" I say aloud. I don't know what else

to do. I miss my friend and my dad misses Grandpa Leo and everything feels wrong.

I hear my dad climb the steps. He walks through each room, checking windows, making sure they're all locked up tight. He stops in my doorway on the way to his room.

"You good, Boog?" he asks. "Need anything?"

"No. I'm okay."

He smiles but his eyes are sad. He walks away before I can say anything else. He goes into his room and I glance at my phone. It's ten. After a little while my eyelids finally start to feel heavy. I pull my covers up and I must fall asleep right away because the next thing I know, I'm opening my eyes in the pitch dark feeling groggy.

I lie quietly, listening to the sleepy sounds of the house. Is my mom home yet? My phone says it's two in the morning, which means she might've come in already. I need to talk to her. I need to ask her what else we can do to help find Aaron and I can't sleep anymore until I do. I roll over onto my side.

Tap . . . tap

I glance at my window. The storm is back. I wait for the tapping to pick up, for the wind to rattle the house . . . but it doesn't. I sit up, swinging my legs over the edge of my bed. I stare up at the ceiling. There's no patter on the roof. There isn't a storm. It's dead quiet.

Tap . . . tap

My heart kicks up and I hold my breath as I step toward

the window. The curtains are closed, but not all the way. A thin strip of the nighttime blackness beyond the glass shows through. I reach toward the curtain to move it aside.

Tap . . . tap

Fear rushes through me. I should run to get my parents. I know I should but I'm too scared to move. My feet feel stuck to the floor. It's like every nerve in my body is awake and on fire, raising my skin to gooseflesh. What is going on here? All I'm doing is opening the curtain. It's probably a bird or a squirrel because it's obviously not the storm and there has to be a simple reason for the tapping. Even in my own head the excuse sounds stupid.

I grip the curtain in my trembling hand, then shove it to the side. The sky is covered in a canopy of patchy clouds that move like giant black shadows across the sky. The moon is half full. I breathe a little easier. I'm all worked up for nothing. There isn't a bird pecking at my window or a squirrel or anything else but then I see something in the yard. I blink a few times to make sure it's not just a trick of the light.

It's not.

It's a person.

CHAPTER 10

I lean in close to the glass, squinting, trying to see through the darkness. The person pulls back their arm and chucks something up at me. It pings off the glass and clatters onto the sill. It's a small piece of gravel.

A wind suddenly whips up, rustling the branches of the downed tree that's still lying on its side in the yard. The person takes several steps away from it. The clouds shift, letting the silver moon light up the shadowy figure for just one second.

Aaron.

I stop breathing. I feel like if I move, he'll disappear. I put my hand, palm slick with sweat, on the glass and stare down at him. He's wearing the same clothes he had on the night he went missing except his pants are torn up at the bottom, his shirt is dirty. His expression sends a chill up my back. He looks scared.

No. Not just scared. Terrified.

"Boog." My dad's voice cuts through the silence. I jump and let out a strangled scream. He rushes over and puts his hands on my shoulders. "Boog? Are you okay?" He glances out the window and I wait for him to notice Aaron, too. But he only looks back at me.

I turn and look at where Aaron had been standing. He's gone.

My dad narrows his gaze at me. "You're scaring me."

"I—I just—I saw—" I can't get the words out.

Did I really see him standing there? That can't be right. He would've gone home, maybe to the police station, or the school. Or he would've come to the front door—something, anything other than just standing in my yard in the middle of the night. My dad waits quietly for me to finish.

"Nothing," I say. "I thought there was another storm starting. I wanted to make sure the window was closed."

His mouth is set in a hard line and I can't tell if he believes me or not. "Why don't you get back into bed. I'll be right back."

I climb back into bed but I don't take my eyes off the window.

A few minutes later my dad comes back with his pillow and a blanket. He makes a little space for himself on the floor and tries to get comfortable.

"What are you doing?" I ask him.

He fluffs up his pillow. "You're shook. I can tell. Don't know why exactly but you've got a lot going on. I'll stay here with you because I know you think you're too much of an almost-teenager to ask me. Get some sleep, Boog."

He lies down and I drape my hand over the side of my bed and wiggle my fingers. Dad takes my hand and squeezes it. I feel better with him there.

I lie awake all night. Either I was seeing things or Aaron is out there, alive, but maybe he's hurt or something, confused. I don't know. I don't understand, but I know I'm going to tell Cedrick and Jules as soon as I get the chance.

"Stop lyin'," Cedrick says to me as we sit, huddled together, in homeroom the next morning. He can't believe what I'm telling him.

"I saw him," I say in a whisper. After thinking about it all night I had made the decision that it had to be him. Nothing else makes sense.

"Why wouldn't he go home?" Jules asks. "My mom was with his mom yesterday, just trying to keep her company. She's so upset."

"I don't know," I say.

"And if he was at your house, why wouldn't he just ring the doorbell?" Cedrick asks.

"You don't believe me?" I ask.

"I believe you," Cedrick says in a way that doesn't convince me he's telling the truth. "It's just really weird. Did you tell your dad?"

"No. I thought maybe it was just my imagination at first." Doubt tries to sneak in but I push it away. I know what I saw. I'm gonna stop trying to convince myself it was something else and instead, get to the bottom of whatever is actually going on.

"We have to tell his mom," Jules says.

"Tell her what?" I ask. "That I saw Aaron outside my house in the middle of the night? That he was throwing gravel at my window? That he didn't even say anything? We can't tell her yet. I need to figure out what's happening."

"How are you gonna do that?" Jules asks.

I shrug. I don't have a solid place to start but I know I can't go to Aaron's mom and tell her I saw her son without any other details.

The day goes by so slow and my sleepless night is making it hard to keep my eyes open by the time the last bell rings. When my mom picks me up, I hop in the van and an awful smell immediately uppercuts my nostrils.

"Mom! What is that smell?"

"I've been cleaning," she says.

I look at the pits of her T-shirt. They don't look sweaty but the inside of the van smells like seventy-eight gym socks mixed with a hint of moldy fruit.

"It's not me," she says, smiling. "'Lita made me a new batch of cleaner."

"I mean, that explains it. You've got dirt on your jeans, too."

"I did some gardening."

I stare blankly at her. My mom is good at lots of things—her job, cooking, helping me with homework—but one thing she doesn't do well is garden. She doesn't have a green thumb at all, and when she and Miss Celia fixed up Cedrick's yard, my mom was relegated to picking out the paving stones and bird bath.

When we pull up to the house I realize that when she said "gardening" she wasn't talking about planting a new rosebush or cutting the grass. She's got dirt pulled up around the entire perimeter of the house and the garage. Off to the side there are three white bags, each the size of a twin mattress.

"Mom?" I ask, a little worried. "What are those?"

"Potting soil," she says. "I'm gonna plant a bunch of flowers. It's gonna so look nice!"

"If you say so," I say under my breath.

She hops out and I follow her inside. I didn't think it was possible for the house to be even more stank than the car but I'm proven wrong the second I step through the door. The smell of 'Lita's cleaning solution hits me in the throat like a punch. Lemon, garlic, and a metallic smell—like wet change.

I have to swallow hard to keep from gagging but spit pools in my mouth. "You said you cleaned but seriously? How can you even breathe in here?"

"We were past due for a deep cleaning," she says, looking

134

around the living room where the curtains are tied up, exposing the windowsills. "It won't hurt you."

"You sure? Because I feel like I'm dying."

Her face twists up. "Don't say that," she says sharply.

"I was just joking." I put my hand on her arm. "You okay?"

She puts her arms around me, hugs me tight. "I'm fine. Just a little tired, and if I'm being honest, a little worried about you. Daddy said something was bothering you last night. Wanna talk about it?"

"Y'all are worried about me but I'm worried about you and Dad."

My mom looks surprised. "Why?"

"It's just Dad was talking about Grandpa Leo and—"

"What?" Mom's voice shoots up an octave. She immediately readjusts herself. "I mean—what did he say about Grandpa?"

"Just that he's missing him and he was thinking about what he might do if he was here."

My mom sighs. "That all?" she asks.

"I mean and the thing about the window." I try to make sure my face doesn't change as I answer her. I'm not sure how much I should say when I'm not 100 percent certain what's going on. "I thought there was another storm starting up. I got up to check the window and Dad scared me. It was late. I'm a little jumpy ever since—ever since—"

"Since Aaron went missing," Mom says. She pulls me closer. "I know it's been rough but we're not giving up, okay? We'll find him." She wipes her eyes with the back of her hand and when I glance up at her, she's crying.

"Mom?" Now feels like the right time to ask about the way she and my dad have been acting. I already asked my dad and his explanation made sense but I'm pretty sure my mom's not thinking of Grandpa Leo right at this moment. "Is there something you're not telling me? Something about Aaron?"

I expect her to laugh it off, to say "of course not" and wave me away but she doesn't. She takes a big breath and blows it out between her teeth.

"Baby," she begins.

My heart crashes inside my chest. She *does* know something and it sounds like she might actually tell me.

"What is it?" I ask. "Please just tell me."

She stares down into my face. "It's nothing. Just worried about you is all." That's not the truth and she knows it. She almost let something slip out but she holds back. "Your dad is working the late shift so it's just you and me tonight. Want pizza or burgers or something else?"

"Burgers sound good," I say. I won't press her. Something's up but whatever it is, she's not ready to let me in on it.

I go up to my room and text Jules.

ME: Something's wrong. I don't know what but my mom is lying to me about something and I think it has to do with Aaron.

JULES: Serious??? Listen. 'Lita's been cleaning all day.

Like spring cleaning. The house smells like somebody's hot breath.

ME: My mom cleaned too. Is this what grown folks do when they're upset about something? Clean?

JULES: LOL maybe. My mom cleans when she's stressed so it kind of makes sense, right?

I add Cedrick to the chat and send him a message.

ME: How are your dads acting? Anything weird?

CEDRICK: I still can't go anywhere. They said they don't want me in the yard till the fence is fixed. And Boog, what the heck is your mom doing in your yard?

ME: Gardening??? IDK why pull up all the dirt if you're just gonna put more dirt back down?

JULES: So we probably shouldn't even try to ask them if we can sleep over, right?

ME: Don't waste your time

CEDRICK: Not gonna happen

ME: This SUCKS and I hate it.

The doorbell rings and I hear my mom open the front door and bring in the food. I toss my phone onto the bed and go downstairs.

"Mom, can Cedrick and Jules come over?"

She looks up at me as she transfers my burger and fries onto a plate. "Not today, Boog." I start to protest but she cuts me off. "I had a late night. I'm gonna go lie down for a little while." She massages her temple as she closes the curtains.

"Everything's locked up. I'll let Daddy in when he gets home." She walks toward the stairs.

"Hey, Mom," I say.

She turns to me. "Boog, I promise if there's something you *need* to know, I'll tell you. But this thing with Aaron has really shaken me." She clenches her teeth. "His poor mother. I cannot imagine—" She stops short and turns away but I can tell she's crying again. She goes up to her room but doesn't close her door.

Nighttime comes while I eat my burger and watch Netflix. I grab a big fluffy blanket off the back of the couch and snuggle up. I'm dozing off before nine and I awake to the darkened TV screen. A little message that reads "Are you still watching?" is dimly lighting the room. I rub my eyes. The house is quiet except for the flush of the AC and the endless chatter of cicadas from outside.

I suddenly feel a little too uneasy to be downstairs by myself. I grab the remote and head upstairs, only hitting the power button when I'm safely at the top. I leave the remote on the top step so that I can take it down in the morning.

In the darkened upstairs hallway, the door to my parents' bedroom sits open. I creep toward it and stand in the doorway for a second. My mom is curled up under a blanket—her breath heavy, her chest rising and falling. She's knocked all the way out.

I turn and head back toward my room when I hear it.

I freeze. Something is pinging against the window in my room.

I glance back at my mom, who doesn't stir. My arms and legs feel heavy as I force myself forward. My chest is tight, blood rushes in my ears. My feet feel like I'm dragging them through quicksand.

In my room, I leave the door open in case I decide to make a quick exit. My heart bangs against my ribs. I gather every little bit of courage I can and push the curtain open. My hands are trembling so bad I almost yank the whole thing off the rod. Bits of gravel bounce off my window.

Tap . . . tap

Aaron is standing by the downed tree.

My legs are moving before I have a chance to think about it. I don't question if I'm really seeing him or not. All I know is that I need to talk to him.

I go downstairs as quickly and quietly as I can. I feel like I can hear everything—my own heartbeat thudding in my ears, the creak of the stairs under my feet, the cicadas screaming. It's too loud and also too quiet.

I need to calm down. Aaron is right down there in the yard. If I can just talk to him, I can ask him what's going on and we can figure it out together.

I tiptoe to the back door, treading so lightly I feel like I'm trying to hover above the floor like a ghost. Through the thick glass of the window in the back door I can see Aaron still standing there. I turn the deadbolt and as it clicks open my entire body tenses. Next is the twist lock on the handle and then the chain. My parents have this thing secured like a bank vault. I wait for a moment to see if Mom will wake up. When I'm sure she's still asleep I grab the handle and twist it—very slowly.

All the things Jules and Cedrick and me had talked about tumble through my head. Why didn't Aaron go home or to the police? Why is he here trying to talk to me? Why doesn't he just come to the door? I turn on the fairy lights my mom has strung up outside, being careful not to hit the switch that controls our new floodlights. Mom would be able to see that from her room. I pull the door open and step onto the back porch. I walk to the edge of the deck but I don't go down the steps into the yard. My gut is telling me not to.

"Aaron?" I whisper.

He takes a step toward me. "Boog."

The nighttime air is warm and thick but a shiver shoots right up my back. His voice is—different. It sounds hollow, empty. He takes another step closer. I try to find his eyes in the shifting shadows but all I can see are two glinting orbs—eyeshine.

"Aaron, what are you doing? Are you okay? What happened to—" I stop. As he steps into the soft glow of the fairy lights, my stomach twists up. I feel sick. Sweat beads on my forehead. I feel afraid. More afraid than I ever have in my whole life. I try to breathe, to calm down, but the fear keeps growing. "Aaron, we gotta call the police. We gotta tell your mom you're okay—" I stop short. "*Are* you okay?"

"No," he says. "I'm not." He looks up at me. His face is

smudged with dirt, he's not wearing any shoes, and his clothes are torn up. There is a dark reddish-brown stain on the collar of his shirt.

"Aaron—what happened to you?"

"Boog, you gotta help me," he says, glancing around. "Something—something happened—is happening—to me." He steps up onto the porch and I take a step back. "I—I don't know what to do. I feel—" He stops, looking down at his bare feet. "What is that?"

"What?" I ask.

Plumes of dark gray smoke stream from the soles of his feet. He hops from one foot to the other.

"What is that?" I ask as I stumble through the open back door of my house. I lose my balance and my feet slip out from under me. I fall hard onto the kitchen floor. Pain rockets through my tailbone.

Aaron stumbles toward me, kicking wildly at the smoke. He rushes forward to try and take cover inside with me and stops so suddenly, it's like he's run into a pane of glass right at the threshold. The door is wide open but he just stops and claps his hand over his nose and mouth. His eyes begin to water and maybe it's a trick of the light, maybe it's me being confused and scared out of my entire mind, but I swear I think I see something red and glistening where his tears should be.

"Aaron?" I ask, my voice shaky and thin. "Aaron, what is going on?"

Smoke continues to billow from his feet and then he turns his head to the side, looks up. I follow his gaze but I don't see anything except the black sky and twinkling stars. He looks back at me.

"Meet me Friday night at City Park. Nighttime. Okay? Please, Boog? Please?"

I don't know if I should say yes. Something is wrong. Something is very, very wrong. I blink to clear my head and he's gone—vanished right in front of me.

A pounding on the stairs startles me and I scramble to my feet as my mom skids into the kitchen.

"Malika, what the—" She's looking at the open door. She glances at me. "Are you hurt?" She grabs me by the shoulder and runs her hand along the side of my neck.

"I—I'm fine. I fell. I thought I saw—" I don't even know what to say. It's not even a convincing lie. I fell and accidentally unlocked the three locks on the back door? I kick myself.

"Mom, I—"

"Go to your room!" she snaps. "Now."

She's so angry but there's also that sadness in her eyes that I can't understand. There's no room for arguing. I go upstairs as she moves to the door and runs her hand along the jamb. I think I hear her exhale as I disappear up the steps.

CHAPTER 11

I sleep but not soundly. I see Aaron's face behind my closed lids. The sound of his voice echoes in my head and I wake up so many times thinking I hear the gravel hitting my window but when I get up to check there's nothing. When the sun slants through my curtains, I accept the fact that I'm not going to get any more sleep and drag myself into the hallway. I hear my dad's voice downstairs and he sounds upset.

"Is that supposed to make me feel better?" he asks.

"The boundary held," my mom says.

"You don't know that," Dad says. "Did she tell you what she saw? Does she even know for sure?"

There is a long pause.

"No," Mom huffs. "Listen, the downed tree is a perfect

excuse to do the work. We need to get it out of the yard as soon as possible, though."

"It'll be gone today," my dad says.

"Will you have enough time to put in the reinforcements before dark?" my mom asks. "I don't want to take any chances."

"I think so," Dad says. "Are you sure you want to do this?"

There is another long period of silence. "I've already begun," says Mom. "I don't think we have a choice. Even if it's for nothing, I'd rather be safe than sorry."

I don't know what boundary my mom's talking about. The fence? It only separates us from Cedrick's yard on that side so getting it fixed shouldn't even be a big deal. Cedrick and his dads are family. All I want to do is talk to Jules and Ced.

I go into the bathroom to brush my teeth and text Jules.

ME: I need to talk to you and Ced ASAP

JULES: Ok

I get dressed and go downstairs. My dad is waiting with his car keys in hand.

"Ready?" he asks. He shoots me a big smile but now he's got that same look on his face as Mom. That scared, worried look.

I nod. I don't see my mom before I leave and that's probably a good thing. She was so mad the night before. My dad drives me to school and drops me off out front.

"Hey, Boog," he says through the open window.

I glance back.

"Be aware of your surroundings today, okay?"

"Um, okay, Dad," I say. He sounds like Mr. Rupert.

He drives off right as Jules and Cedrick get there. I grab them both by the arm and pull them inside.

"What is going on?" Cedrick asks. "My dads were up all night. Walking around the house like they were on patrol or something."

"My mom, too," says Jules.

I pull them against the lockers in A building and they huddle in. "Listen. Something happened last night and I don't even know how to tell you what it was."

"Tell us, Boog," says Ced. "Because something is goin' on and I feel like it's bad. Not just regular bad either. It feels like it's something terrible."

I take a deep breath and lower my voice to a whisper. "I saw Aaron again."

Jules and Cedrick freeze. I think they even stop breathing for a minute.

"What do you mean you saw him?" Jules asks. "Everybody thinks he's—well—you know what they think."

"They think he's dead," Cedrick says.

"He's not," I say. "I saw him. And it wasn't my imagination or a dream or anything like that. I saw him. He was in my yard in the middle of the night. He threw something at my window to get my attention and I went down and opened the back door."

"You went out?" Jules gawks at me. "At night?"

Cedrick shakes his head. "I bet your parents *loved* that."

"What was I supposed to do? I saw him out there and he looked scared to death. I talked to him. He said something happened to him but he couldn't say what. He had on the same clothes, no shoes, and when he tried to come in, he just stopped. I blinked and he was gone. Just disappeared." I think of telling them about the smoke I saw billowing from Aaron's feet, but the thing is—I'm terrified of what that could mean. So much so that I don't want to say what I'm thinking. Not yet.

Cedrick's breath catches and he leans close to me. "What? He disappeared? How?"

"Just like I said. He was gone." I snap my fingers. "Like that." I lean against the locker. "He asked me to meet him at the park Friday night."

Jules crosses their arms and huffs. "Like, in the actual night? Nighttime?"

"If he said night, Jules, that means at night," Cedrick says. "Dang."

Jules rolls their eyes.

Cedrick puts his hands up. "I'm just sayin'."

"I'm going." I make up my mind right there. No more guessing at what's going on. I'm gonna find out and I'm gonna help Aaron.

"How?" asks Jules. "You can't just walk out of your house. Your mom and dad would never let you go."

"I can do it," I say. "My mom is gonna put me on punishment till I die if she finds out but I gotta go. I have to try and help him."

"Help him do what?" Cedrick asks. "Why doesn't he just go home?"

I don't want to say what I'm thinking.

"I'm coming, too," Jules says, resting their hand on my arm.

Cedrick looks like he's completely done with the both of us.

"I'm going to ask to go to the skate rink at five. If they can take us." I glance at Jules and they nod. "Then we can sneak out, go to the park, which is, like, a fifteen-minute walk, meet Aaron, and get back before they find out."

"Sounds dumb," says Ced. "Real dumb."

"You know you're going, too, so I don't know why you're acting like this," Jules says.

"Whatever," Cedrick says, crossing his arms hard over his chest. "Our parents are not going to take us back to the place where Aaron went missing."

He's right but I can't think of another place that'll put us within walking distance of City Park. My plan isn't great but it's all we've got.

"So, we meet up at your house so we can get dropped off together?" Cedrick asks.

I grin and he tries his hardest not to do the same. Like Jules said, he's gonna go along with whatever plan we come up with no matter how unlikely it is to actually succeed.

"Our parents are gonna kill us," Cedrick says.

"At least we'll be ghosts together, too," I say. "We'll be the ghost squad." I laugh just so I don't have to think about how close that might be to the truth.

On Friday, every class feels like it's three hours long. Staying focused is a problem. I haven't even asked my parents if we can go to the skating rink yet but if I ask them too far ahead of time and they say yes, they might change their minds so I leave it to the last minute. My mom's still upset after what happened at the back door so I don't know if I'm in a position to be asking for anything but I have to try.

After my last class, I wait with Jules and Cedrick for our parents to pick us up and as soon as my mom pulls up, we all pile into the car together.

"Wait a minute," Mom says. "Jules, your mama know you're riding home with me?"

"Yes, ma'am," says Jules. "I texted her."

My mom looks at Ced. "And you?"

"My dad told me to say thank you and that he'll pick us all up next week to give you a break."

My mom huffs. "Y'all are scheming and I don't like it."

"Scheming?" The tone I'm going for is sweet and innocent but I think I sound suspicious and sneaky. "Us?"

Mom eyes me in the rearview mirror. "Mmmhmm."

"You're right," I say.

Jules and Cedrick whip their heads around to look at me.

"We want to go skating." I decide to just put this part of it out there. "Can we go? Please?"

Jules shakes their head and Cedrick just turns and stares out the window.

"Skating?" Mom levels her eyes with the road. "I don't know—"

"Please, Mom," I say. "I gotta get out of the house. We all do. We're sick of being on lockdown."

"Just trying to keep y'all safe," my mom says, an edge to her tone. "But you insist on making that hard for me to do."

I lean forward and gently put my hands on her shoulders. "Please? I know you're mad—"

"Not mad," she says. "Concerned."

"I'm sorry. I really mean it."

She pats my hand. "I know it's hard to be cooped up in the house and I'm not against y'all getting out but the skating rink is where Aaron went missing. I'm not sure I'm comfortable with that."

"I've been thinking about that," I say honestly. "But we've been going to that rink since we were little. You and Daddy used to go all the time, too. It used to be the spot—*our* spot. It's not fair that we can't go back."

Mom sighs. "I understand all of that, baby. I really do. And I want y'all to have some fun. Y'all can go."

I grab Jules's arm and squeeze it tight.

"With a few stipulations," Mom says quickly. "Daddy will take you and pick you up. You will keep your location on and you don't leave the rink with anybody but Daddy, got it?"

I'm already thinking of how that's not going to work but I agree to everything just so we can have the chance to go. I have to find out what's going on with Aaron and as soon as I know, I'll tell her. And if I'm being real, I think about how she's not being honest with me about a lot of stuff right now. The weird phone calls and hushed conversations—I don't like that either but she says it's for a reason, and I feel the same way about what I need to do.

When we pull up to the house there's a beat-up old green pickup truck in the driveway and three people are standing in the side yard cutting the fallen tree into pieces. My dad rolls a part of the tree trunk behind the house.

"What's he gonna do with that?" I ask.

Mom shrugs. "I'm not sure. He said he wants to make me a table or something."

"I've never seen him make anything out of wood in my whole life," I say. "He knows how to do that?"

She laughs. "I don't think so, but if he wants to try to build something we'll let him. Can't hurt, right? Go inside and let me talk to him about takin' y'all to the rink."

We go in and put our bags in the entryway. As I walk through the kitchen, the mail sits in a pile on the island and something catches my eye—a piece of paper with a strange symbol at the top. I pick it up and take a closer look.

"What's that?" Jules asks, peering over my shoulder. "Is that a tombstone?"

The symbol at the top of the page looks like a grave marker and on its face it reads **VDS, Est. 1901** in bold black lettering.

"It's an invoice," I say.

VDS, Est. 1901

CONSECRATED EARTH.	100 POUNDS.	QUANTITY 3.

I hand it to Jules. "Consecrated earth?"

They pass it to Ced whose mouth forms a little o. "Grave-yard dirt."

"What?" I ask.

Ced sighs. "I know I'm the class clown but do y'all pay attention to anything Mr. Keller says? Like, at all?"

I take the paper from him and set it back on the counter. "It has my house as the delivery address."

"And your mom has been *gardening*," Jules says. "So has my mom."

I position the paper back on the counter so that it looks like I never touched it, then I nudge Jules and Ced toward the stairs. We go down and close the door behind us.

"Our parents are vampire-proofing," I say.

Cedrick inhales so hard he almost chokes on his own spit. "What? No. You really think so?"

I nod. "Consecrated earth? Weird lights on the porch? This new lock-up-everything-in-sight routine? C'mon. What else could it be?"

"Why, though?" Jules asks. "What made them decide to go to the trouble? The only place I've ever heard of that still uses graveyard dirt is the old hospital in San Marcos."

"They're out in the boonies, that's why," says Cedrick.

"This is all because Aaron went missing," I say.

"Well, he's not missing anymore, right?" says Jules. "Maybe when our parents see him, they'll realize how ridiculous this is and they can chill out."

"I don't know," I say. "For right now, let's just figure out how we're gonna meet Aaron. We'll find out what's going on and go right back to the rink. Then we can decide what to tell everybody."

"Should we take some mace or something?" Jules asks. "Lita has a stun gun."

"Why?" Cedrick asks. "Why does she have that? She barely goes anywhere."

Jules shrugs. "She says you can never be too careful. Want me to grab it?"

"Do we even know how to use it?" I picture myself accidentally electrocuting Cedrick and immediately dismiss the idea. "No way. But maybe we should take something else." I glance toward the basement pantry.

"Garlic?" Cedrick asks. "What for?" He looks at me quizzically and then his face shifts into an expression of confusion. "Boog. What are you not telling us?"

"I—I don't know." I don't want to tell him what I'm thinking. I need more than just my overactive imagination to confirm the creeping suspicion I have. "Look, we don't need to take anything. Let's just get ready to go."

I stick my phone in my back pocket and I make sure the lens my mom bought me is attached. We head back upstairs just as my mom is coming in the front door.

"Dad's ready whenever you are," she says. She slips me ten dollars and cups my face in her hands. "Be careful and don't do anything that'll make me regret this."

I give her a hug and press my face into her shoulder so she can't see my terrified expression. "We'll be okay, Mom. Promise."

We throw on our shoes and meet my dad in the driveway.

"Mom says you need a ride to the rink," he says. "I'll drop y'all off and be back at six."

"Six? Dad, we're not babies," I say. Six o'clock isn't enough time. "And we've been in the house for a week. Can we stay till eight?"

"Seven," he says.

"Seven fifty?" I ask, giving him my best sad-puppy-dog eyes.

"Seven forty-five and this isn't a negotiation. Take it or leave it."

"I mean it sounds like a negotiation," Cedrick says under his breath.

"Seven forty-five is perfect." I don't know if Aaron will think seven o'clock counts as nighttime but that's gonna have to work. I try to calculate if we'll have enough time to get to the park and back. No matter what, we'll be cutting it close.

Jules, Cedrick, and I sit in the back of my dad's SUV as he steers us toward the rink. It's five thirty when he drops us off. There are only a few people hanging around. The lights are low and the rink is lit up by the glittering ball in the center of the ceiling. It's just like it was the night of the fundraiser only there is hardly anybody here. The nervous flutter that has kept my stomach in knots all day kicks up.

"Maybe we should skate for a little while," Jules says.

"Nah. We need to give my dad enough time to leave, then we gotta head out so we can meet him back here."

"Are we even sure this is a good idea?" Cedrick asks. I can see that he's second guessing everything and I don't blame him. "You saw Aaron and he wants you to meet him—at night. But he won't just go home and talk to his mom? It sounds weird to me."

Jules nods. "Yeah, but why? Why is he acting like that?"

"You don't have to come with me," I say. "I get it if you're scared."

"I'm not scared," Cedrick says quickly.

"I am," I say. "I really am. Something is happening here but Aaron's our friend. I want him back. I gotta go talk to him." I almost say aloud the thing that's been gnawing at me ever since I saw that brown stain on Aaron's shirt and the way his eyes glinted in the dark.

I glance at my phone again. It's five forty-five. My dad's been gone for fifteen minutes. He should be back home by now. "We have two hours. Let's go to the park and just wait. If he shows up, great. If not, we'll come back and figure something else out."

"Hold up," Jules says. "Your mom said to keep your location on. What if she looks at it and sees that we're in the park?"

I don't know how to get around that. The location has to be off, at least for a little bit.

"Ced, keep your location on and put your phone in a locker."

"Why I gotta leave my phone here?" he asks, his bottom lip poking out.

"Don't pout," Jules says. "It's not cute."

"I'm not worried about being cute. I'm worried somebody's going to steal my phone and I have top-tier memes saved on there."

"Nobody wants your first-generation iPhone, Ced," Jules says.

Cedrick puts his hand on his chest like he's actually wounded. "It's better than that flip phone my dads were making me carry around last year. Y'all remember that? The only game on there was *Snake*."

"Umm, what?" Jules asks.

"Focus, please," I say impatiently. "Ced, please. Leave it here. We'll lock it up."

Cedrick begrudgingly puts his phone in a locker and I pay a dollar in quarters to lock it. I take out my phone and turn off the location. Not a minute later my mom is texting me.

MOM: Turn on your location.

ME: It is.

I turn on the location for a minute, then turn it back off.

MOM: It's popping up and then disappearing.

ME: Can you check Ced's location? We're all right here.

There's a pause.

MOM: Ethan sees it. Just stay together please. I'll see if we can get your phone looked at.

ME: Ok. Luv u.

MOM: Love you

I hate lying to her. It makes me feel awful, but I just keep telling myself it's for a good reason. I turn to Ced and Jules. "Okay. Let's go."

Cedrick and Jules trail behind me as I walk to the front doors. I stop dead in my tracks as soon as I get a glimpse of the parking lot. My dad is still out there. He's just sitting in the car with the engine off. He's looking down at something in his lap, probably his phone. His face is lit up by the cool blue flicker from the screen. I duck back inside, pushing Jules and Cedrick against the wall.

"My dad's still here!"

"Oh, you thought this was gonna be easy?" Cedrick says. "Come on, Boog. Look how they've been acting since Aaron went missing. They're scared the same thing's gonna happen to us. And here we are, skating around in the exact same place he went missing at. Of course he's waiting out there. I'm surprised he didn't come in and post up at one of the tables."

"We can try to go out the back," Jules offers.

"See?" I say, giving Jules a wide grin. "I see who's really on my side."

"You gon' be on the *in*side of your room for the rest of your natural life if we get found out," Cedrick says. He's whispering like my dad can hear him across the parking lot.

"Are you coming or not?" I ask him.

He sighs and shuffles along behind me as we look for the rear door. The bright green exit sign lights up a short hallway near the back of the rink. I look to see if an alarm will go off if I open it like the exit doors in the gym at school. I don't see anything saying it will. I rest my hand on the door and gently push it open. No alarm sounds and Cedrick and Jules squeeze out behind me. We stand in the alley behind the rink as the sky turns a hazy orange high above our heads. It's now or never.

CHAPTER 12

Six o'clock.

We have an hour and forty-five minutes to do what we can to help Aaron and get back without my parents finding out.

The narrow alley behind the rink runs the entire length of the building. Going right will take us back to the parking lot where my dad is waiting. Left will take us behind a Dillard's and a restaurant in the direction of City Park.

At any other time, Cedrick would be thinking up every way this could go wrong and telling us loudly how much trouble we'll be in if we get caught, and Jules would give him a hard time for being so worried. But it's not like that. We're quiet the entire way. Scared, but way too curious to stop. It takes us twenty minutes to get to the park.

I used to come here all the time with my parents. The

playground was new when I was five, but now it's kind of run-down. But the equipment wasn't the best part even when it was new. The best part is the big expanse of green that surrounds it. The tall trees with their wide leaves and thick branches always gave us the perfect amount of shade in the sweltering Texas summer.

As we approach the park, I realize we're basically alone. A few people are jogging. A few others are walking their dogs along the track that runs around the entire perimeter. They're minding their own business and clearing out altogether as the sun starts to dip.

Long shadows grow all around us. I check my phone. Six twenty-eight. The sun disappears below a horizon I can't see and a wash of inky blackness pulls itself across the sky. Jules takes a step toward me. Cedrick is already gripping the back of my shirt.

I can't believe I'm out here in the dark like this. It is literally my parents' worst nightmare, the thing they taught me to avoid at almost any cost.

"Boog?" says a voice.

Cedrick gasps. He's looking past me and I turn to see something emerging from the deepest shadows cast by the towering oak trees.

Jules stumbles back as Aaron steps out.

"I—I didn't think you'd come," he says, that weird tremble in his voice; that hollow sound I'd heard before fills me with dread. "Please," he says, like he can tell how afraid I am. "Please don't be scared of me."

"I don't want to be scared of you, Aaron." It's like what I'm seeing doesn't match my gut reaction. I can see Aaron—my friend—standing right in front of me and still every single cell in my body is screaming at me to be afraid. I'm terrified. But there's something else under all that fear. The hair on the back of my neck is standing straight up. I have the same feeling I had when I stepped out onto the porch to talk to Aaron the night before. Something deep in the pit of my stomach is telling me to run—or to fight.

"Boog," Aaron says, his eyes glinting in the dark. "I'm really happy you're here."

I gather myself and take a step toward him. He backs up.

"Don't come too close," he says. "I—I don't think it's safe."

"Why?" Jules asks. They stand next to me, their shoulder pressed against mine. They're trembling and so am I.

"Something happened to me," says Aaron.

"That night at the skating rink," I say.

He nods.

"Have you talked to your mom?" Cedrick asks. He's pushed aside his fears, too, and is standing on the other side of me. "She's worried about you."

"I can't," says Aaron. He shakes his head. "Not yet."

"What are you waiting for?" Jules asks. "People have been

looking for you. Some people think you're—well—they think you're dead."

Aaron raises his head and locks eyes with me. I don't know if it's a trick of the shadows, maybe the angle of his head, I don't know—but his eyes look bigger, wider, and I realize that it's because I don't see any of the white. They're mostly black, flecked with tiny dots of red. Jules must see it at the same time because they grip my arm so hard, I almost yell.

"I went to the bathroom," Aaron says. "That night at the rink . . . someone came in after me." He takes a step forward, lowering his eyes. "Then I think they hit me or something. Right in the back of my head. Next thing I know I'm in the alley out back leaning up against the side of the building and—and—" His voice catches.

My breaths come in short quick bursts, like I can't get enough air. That impossible thing that's been sitting inside my head since I first saw him in my yard is true. I know it. But I wait for him to say it.

"Someone bit me." Aaron touches the side of his neck, just above the dark stain on his collar. "Right here."

We don't say anything. We don't move.

I take a step closer to him. "Someone bit you? Like, a person?"

Aaron nods. "I don't know who it was, or why, but I think I must have passed out. Then when I woke up here, in the park, I felt like I got hit by a truck. Every muscle in my body felt like it was on fire. My throat burned." He clenches his fist near his neck, then lets his hand drop to his side. He glances up at me. "I know how it sounds. It sounds crazy."

I open my mouth to speak but Cedrick beats me to it. "Anything else bothering you?" He looks Aaron over from head to toe. "How do you feel in the daytime? What about old scars or scrapes?"

Cedrick knows something.

"When I was ten," Aaron says, "I broke my pinkie finger and they had to put me to sleep so they could put a pin in it. That's how it feels in the daytime. Like I want to stay awake but I just can't. And the sun, it doesn't actually burn me but it feels like that, like my skin is on fire. And that scar where I got my finger fixed? It's gone now. So is every other scar from every single other time I scraped my knee or my elbow. They're all gone now."

I can hear Cedrick's breathing. It's slowed down, like he's calm. He steps in front of me. "Boog, gimme your phone."

"What? Why?"

"Please don't call anybody," Aaron says.

"I'm not," says Cedrick. "I just wanna see somethin'."

I hand him my phone. He points it at Aaron and snaps a picture. The flash lights up the dark for a split second. Aaron stands unnaturally still. Like he's not even breathing.

Cedrick looks at the screen and lets the air hiss out from between his teeth. He hands it back to me. Jules and I look down at the screen together. Aaron's dirty T-shirt and tattered jeans are hanging in the photo but I don't see Aaron at all. He's not there.

My hand begins to shake so violently that if there are any other clues in the photo, we don't catch them.

"I'm not there, am I?" Aaron asks. "And there's one other thing." He rests his hand on the left side of his chest—over his heart. "I can't feel it beating."

Jules is on the verge of tears. Cedrick is just staring at the ground. Aaron hangs his head and begins to sob. Little rivulets of crimson liquid stream from his eyes and he tries to turn his face away so I can't see.

This is Aaron.

I push aside the stifling fear and walk straight up to him. He doesn't back away this time. I reach out, slowly, and put my arms around him. He is cold as the inside of our fridge and the angles of his lanky frame feel too sharp. I rest my head against his chest.

His heart isn't beating.

Aaron is a vampire.

CHAPTER 13

I should run. Everything in me is telling me to. I should get as far away from him as I can but I don't. This is Aaron. My new friend, and I can't let him figure this out alone. I raise my head and look at him. "I'm going to help you. I promise."

Bloody tears slide down his cheeks and he pulls his shirt up to wipe his face. He takes a deep breath and the air he blows out is icy. "Whoever bit me was at the skating rink that night," he says. "They had to be. I need to find them and make them undo this." He opens and closes his hands in front of him. "And we have to make sure they can't do this to anyone else."

A new fear creeps into my mind. I've been so worried about Aaron, I haven't stopped to seriously consider that *we* might be in real danger, too. Will the vamp who bit Aaron come after us now that we know what happened? Panic catches me in a vise grip.

Aaron shakes his head. "You can't say anything to anyone."

"We have to tell somebody," Jules says. "Somebody has to be able to help us."

"No," Aaron says forcefully. "You can't tell anyone. I have to find out who did this to me and I need your help."

"Boog," Cedrick says. "It's seven ten."

I don't want to leave Aaron but I have to get back to the rink before my dad goes in to find me.

I grab Aaron's hand, ignoring how cold it is. "It's going to be okay. Can you come to my house tomorrow?"

"Tomorrow night, maybe. But I don't know if I should. Did you see all that smoke? And I couldn't actually go into your house. I just couldn't."

"You don't have to be scared," I say.

"It's not that. It's—"

"Boog, we gotta go," Jules says.

I squeeze Aaron's hand one more time. "How can I find you again? What if I need to talk to you?"

"I'll come back to your house as soon as I can." He steps into the shadow of an oak tree and disappears.

Jules lets out a high-pitched yelp as they yank me backward. My legs are wobbly underneath me and my head is spinning.

"Oh my god, Boog," Jules says frantically. "You know what this means? Boog. You *know* what this means."

"I—I can't believe this," I say in a whisper.

"Less talk, more running," Cedrick says. "We're gonna get in so much trouble if we don't get back."

We race to the rink but it feels like we're running away from everything we just saw, running away from Aaron. As we cut through the park and head back to the skate rink the dark feels closer. I run faster than I ever have in my life. We scramble behind the building and pull on the handle to the rear door. It's locked.

"We didn't prop it open?" Cedrick asks.

"Did you tell somebody to?" Jules asks, annoyed.

"Come on," I say, leading them to the front of the building. I stop and peer around the corner. My dad is out of the car, walking up to the front of the rink.

"Oh no," Jules says quietly.

We duck back behind the building and panic starts to set in. I try to think straight. "Okay. Follow me."

I walk slowly to the front door. My dad has his back to us just inside the entryway. I walk up behind him and Cedrick's eyes open wide. He mouths, *what are you doing?* I mouth back, *play along.* I jump up and throw my arms around my dad's neck.

He spins around and I laugh the fakest laugh ever. Cedrick and Jules laugh, too. Also fake. This is why we're friends. They play along even when they don't know what's happening.

My dad puts his hands on his knees. "Y'all scared me half to death. You lucky I'm not your mama. She might've swung on y'all."

"Dang, really?" I say.

"What were y'all doing?" my dad asks. "I didn't even see you when I walked in."

Cedrick shoots me a quick glance. "Me and Jules had a bet that you'd never let somebody sneak up on you, so Boog decided to try it."

My dad looks a little surprised but then he smiles. "Y'all are real sweaty. Smells like alligator kneecaps."

Now we're all laughing for real.

"Let's go," says my dad. "It's late and y'all need a shower, maybe some bleach."

"I left my phone," Cedrick says.

He immediately clamps his mouth shut. I wait for my dad to ask why it's in a locker and not in his pocket but he just laughs.

"Well, run and get it," my dad says. "Phones are expensive. You can't just leave it lying around."

"Oh, don't worry, Mr. Wilson," Jules says. "Ced couldn't give that phone away."

"Can't be that bad," my dad says.

Cedrick runs to grab his phone and when he comes back my dad looks at the phone, then grins. "Cedrick, this thing belongs in a museum. Does it even work?"

Cedrick shrugs. "It's better than the flip phone."

My dad puts his arm around me and points at Cedrick. "You're absolutely right."

We pile into the car and drive home. My dad sings along to a song on the radio as me, Jules, and Ced breathe a collective sigh of relief. Our plan worked this time, but we cut it way too close.

When we pull up to the house my dad parks in the garage. As we pile out, I notice a big blue tarp covering something in the corner. Power tools are scattered across the workbench and there are wood chips and sawdust everywhere.

"Are you almost done with the new table?" I ask.

My dad looks confused. "The what?"

I pause for a minute. "Uh, never mind. I saw the sawdust and I thought Mom said something about you making a table."

His expression doesn't change. "Oh right. I'm almost done. I'm sure your mom's gonna hate it but I bet you any amount of money she'll tell me it's the best table she's ever had."

"She's gonna be supportive but I'm gonna tell you the truth. If it's ugly we can't keep it."

My dad laughs lightly, draping his arm around my shoulders as we leave through the side door of the garage and he locks the door behind us.

"Y'all can stay over," my dad says to Jules and Ced. "I know it's been rough here recently, with Aaron going missing." He stops and stares directly at me for a split second, then looks away. "It's been hard to deal with something that just doesn't make sense. A little downtime will do all of y'all some good. Just make sure you shower because I can't have my house smellin' like Fritos and booty sweat. What were y'all doin' anyway? Speed skating?"

"I should probably run home and get some clothes," Cedrick says, changing the subject.

My dad glances out the window and draws his mouth into a tight line. "It's dark, Ced. I got some sweats you can borrow. You can go get some clothes tomorrow. You good with that?"

"Yes, sir," Cedrick says.

We wash off the funk and I let Jules wear a pair of my shorts and a *Stranger Things* T-shirt I found at the mall. Cedrick gets a T-shirt that belongs to my mom and a pair of Green Bay Packers pajama pants. I can't even look at Jules or Ced because all I want to do is talk about what we saw but we can't. Not in front of my dad.

We drag blankets and pillows to the basement and my dad goes through his nightly routine, locking up everything like a vault before sending down popcorn and drinks. I listen closely— the distinct creak of the third step going upstairs, the softer groan of the landing, and then finally a whirring in the wall as he turns on the water in the bathroom.

I lean in close to Jules and Ced. "You know what this means, right? You know what Aaron is now?"

Cedrick looks down into his lap, shaking his head. "I don't even know how to tell you what I'm thinking," he says. "I don't even know if it's real but you saw him—he didn't show up in the picture, the sun makes him knock out. Come on. You tell me what that sounds like to y'all."

Jules presses their lips together. None of us wants to say it but I can't deny it anymore.

"He's a vampire," I say quietly. Saying the word makes

me shiver. That's how I know it's true. My gut is telling me it is.

Cedrick leans back and Jules tilts their head to look up at the ceiling.

"No," they say. "Vampires are extinct."

"Jules, c'mon," I say. "It can't be anything else."

"You saw his neck," says Cedrick. "That was blood on his collar. And I know you heard his voice. You can't tell me it wasn't a vampire voice."

Jules levels their eyes at him. "A vampire voice? What does that even mean?"

"You know what it means," Cedrick says.

"Nope. I really, really don't," says Jules.

"You knew what questions to ask," I say to Cedrick. "You already sound like you've got your mind made up." Cedrick is the one always telling us how our parents need to ease up on the vampire-proofing and the extra safety stuff. So I'm a little confused by how he knew just what to ask and why he was so calm while he was questioning Aaron.

"Did you know my dads put a library next to their lab in the basement?" Cedrick asks.

We aren't allowed in Cedrick's basement because his dads are engineers and they have a home lab down there with a bunch of really expensive stuff. They even have a little keypad on the basement door where you have to punch in a number to open it.

I wrap myself in a blanket. "How do you know that? We're not even allowed down there."

"We're also not allowed to be out after it gets dark but we sure were in the park, breaking ten different rules." He smiles. "I saw them take down bookshelves and a bunch of boxes full of dusty books they said they found at a thrift store. So I went to see for myself. I know the code to the door and everything."

"You're real proud of yourself, huh?" I ask.

"What does this have to do with how you knew so much about what is happening with Aaron?" Jules asks. "That stuff about the scars? We all know vampires could heal but I've never even thought of scars or injuries they might've had before they were turned. Where's that come from?"

"I'm getting to that part," Ced says. "So I went down to the basement when my dads were busy and—"

"What kind of stuff do they have?" Jules asks. "Like robots and stuff?"

"They have a drone and a bunch of other gadgets," Cedrick says. "I went down thinking maybe they'd have some old comics mixed in with the books. They didn't." He rolls his eyes. "But I was looking at the other books and guess what almost every single one of them was about?" He raises one bushy eyebrow. "Vampires."

"Really?" I ask.

"Yeah," says Cedrick. "And not Dracula or Blade or those sparkly vegetarian ones either. I mean some of the books down there look like the ones they keep under the glass at the library. They're old. Some of them were falling apart. They're about all kinds of bloodsucking creatures from all over the world—strigoi, vrykolakas, penanggalan."

"I've never heard of those," Jules says. "There were that many different kinds of vamps?"

Cedrick nods.

"Why do your dads have so many books about vampires?" I ask.

"I don't know," says Cedrick. "But that's where I got the questions. There's all kinds of stuff about North American vamps. There's lists of what they were like and what they could do."

"Okay, so your dads have books about vampires," says Jules. "That doesn't mean Aaron is one."

"Then you tell me why he wanted to meet after it was dark," Cedrick says. "Why he says he can't go home. Why he says someone bit him and now his skin feels like it's burning when he's out in the sun. He can't keep his eyes open in the daytime. And I don't know if y'all caught this, but he was scared he was gonna hurt us. He knows he's dangerous now."

Jules just doesn't want to believe it. I don't think any of us do. Vampires have been extinct since the Reaping. Everyone knows that. We learn about their extinction. We celebrate it every year, but we can't deny what we've all seen with our own eyes.

"Who's dangerous?" My mom is suddenly standing on the bottom step.

We all exchange quick glances and I jump up to hug her.

"Nothing," I say. "We're gonna watch *Underworld* and we were just talking about vampires."

"Is that right?" she says, her eyebrow raised. "What were y'all talking about?"

"Cedrick thinks maybe there's still some vamps lurking around somewhere," I say. Cedrick glares at me.

Mom huffs out a quick laugh. "Aren't y'all the ones always telling me I need to let the past go? Now you're wondering if they're still out there?"

"What do you think, Mrs. Wilson?" Jules says. "You think vampires could still exist?"

My mom tilts her head to the side and sighs. "I don't know what you want me to say, baby. I'm confident the Vanquishers wiped them out but"—she pauses—"but I don't see anything wrong with taking a few extra precautions."

Like consecrated earth? I think to myself.

"Dinner will be ready soon," Mom says as she turns and goes back upstairs. "Make sure y'all wash up."

We wait for her to move out of earshot, then lower our voices to a whisper.

"So what do we do now?" I ask. "I told Aaron I would help him and I meant it."

"We gotta find out who bit him," Cedrick says.

"Why?" Jules asks.

"Because," says Cedrick. "In one of those books it says if you find the vampire who bit you, and kill it, you can go back to normal or something like that."

I try to think if I've heard that in any of my classes. I know I've seen it in movies. There's always a hunt for the head vampire and somehow killing it magically frees anyone they've turned from the curse of vampirism. I don't know if I believe that or not but we don't have much else to go on. What we learn in school is a pretty clear-cut picture of what vampires were but we definitely don't learn about how to reverse the effects of a vampire's bite. Honestly, our Vampire History class is more about celebrating the Vanquishers and the Reaping than anything else.

"Can you get us one of those books?" I ask. "I think we should look at it."

Cedrick nods.

"And we're gonna do what—hunt down a vampire and kill it?" Jules asks in a whisper. "We don't even know who it was. It could be anybody. And I don't know if you noticed but we're not exactly vampire-hunting material."

"How you figure?" Cedrick asks. "The Vanquishers were just normal people like your grandma. She doesn't have any special powers. She's just somebody who wanted to help people. We can do that, too."

He's right but Jules isn't convinced.

"Look," I say. "Let's just think about this. Whoever it is has to be somebody who was at the rink the night of the fundraiser and that means it's probably somebody from our school."

"A student?" Cedrick asks, eyes wide. "You think we're in school with a vampire? I thought they sleep in the daytime? You heard what Aaron said."

Jules pulls their blanket close.

I turn to Cedrick. "We need that book from your house. And in the meantime I think we should talk to Aaron's mom."

"Aaron said not to tell anybody," Jules says.

"I know, but maybe we can just go over, tell her we're gonna figure this out." I know it doesn't make sense. I can't tell her about Aaron. She'll think I've lost my whole mind. But I want to at least see her. "Tomorrow," I say. "You'll get one of those books and then we'll go talk to her."

CHAPTER 14

The next morning my mom makes breakfast and we eat before Jules and Cedrick go home to change and my dad sits down at the table with me and Mom.

Mom sets her hands on the table and there's an awkward silence before she turns to me. "I need to talk to you about something."

I glance up at her, then at my dad. Do they know I left the rink? My life flashes before my eyes.

Mom folds her hands in front of her. Her face is deadly serious. "Boog, the other night when I came in the kitchen and the back door was open—I need you to tell me what you saw."

I stare into my plate. "I mean, I opened the door but I didn't see anything."

"Why did you open it?" Mom asks.

I look toward my dad, who is way too quiet.

"I just wanted to stand on the porch," I lie. "I've been stuck inside since Aaron went missing. I'm sorry, I know the rules, I just—"

"Decided you'd break them?" my mom asks. She's not mad. Her voice is low, calm. She's genuinely asking.

"I'm sorry, Mom," I say. "I know you're worried about us after what happened with Aaron."

She glances at my dad and something silent passes between them.

"I love you," Mom says. "I love Jules and Cedrick and their families, too. I don't want anything to happen to any of you."

"I know," I say. I can't be all the way honest. Not yet. When I know more, when I find out what's really going on, I'll tell her and my dad everything.

"I'll ease up a little, okay?" she asks.

A wave of guilt crashes over me. I'm lying to her and she's buying it and now she feels bad for being so hard on me. All I've ever wanted was to be like the other kids at my school, to have the same kind of freedom everybody else has but now I don't want it. There *is* something to be afraid of . . . something to be *terrified* of.

"Jules and Ced can come over whenever, just like before," she says. "No more staying in the house all the time."

"Really?" I ask.

"Yes. Nothing's changing in the house, though. We still

lock up. We still need to know who's coming over. But I'm gonna try to give you a little more leeway." She smiles. "Just keep your phone on, check in, and tell me if you see anything suspicious."

My dad winces, then tries to act like he didn't.

My mom clears her throat. "I mean if you see somebody new hanging around or maybe trying to talk to you—"

"Like Mr. Rupert?" I ask. "He's the only creep I can think of."

My dad laughs. "Okay. Let's move on." He squeezes my mom's hand. "What are you and your little friends getting into today?"

"I don't know yet," I say. "As much trouble as possible, I think."

"Very funny," Mom says as she gets up and my dad clears the table. "I already talked to Ced's dads and Jules's mama. We're all on the same page, so please don't try to be slick."

I jump up and give her a hug, then run to get dressed and head next door to find Jules.

'Lita opens the door. She's got her salt-and-pepper hair pulled into a long braid down her back. She's in her sixties and Miss Celia looks just like her. Jules favors them both so much.

"Bendicion, 'Lita," I say. I don't speak Spanish very well but Jules's mom taught me this and 'Lita lights up when I say it.

"Dios te bendiga," she says, smiling. "You're getting better and better at that. Come in. Jules is in the front room." She kisses me on both cheeks as I slip off my shoes.

I go into the living room where Jules is dusting the mantel over their fireplace. Music is booming from somewhere in the back. The scent of the homemade cleaner, the same recipe my mom uses, hangs in the air.

"What's your housecleaning music, Boog?" Jules asks. "Like, what do you hear and you just know—oop—time to clean?"

"I mean, you know how my mom is. It's Mary J. Blige and Beyoncé or nothin'. But my dad is on some other stuff lately."

Jules tilts their head. "Like what?"

"He's big into show tunes right now. Especially *Shrek the Musical*."

"Shrek has a musical?"

I laugh as I picture my dad singing along.

"Think we can convince 'Lita to listen to some Beyoncé?" Jules steps toward me and looks me dead in the eye. "If I have to listen to one more Tito Nieves song, I'm gonna lose it."

"I can change it to Gilberto Santa Rosa or Gran Combo de Puerto Rico," 'Lita says as she joins us in the living room. "Who do you like better?"

Jules shrugs. "How about Bad Bunny?"

'Lita looks like she's personally offended by the suggestion. "How about no?" She grumbles something under her breath as she disappears down the hallway. Miss Celia lugs an ancient-looking vacuum cleaner over and sits it in front of Jules, who just frowns.

"Hey, Boogie," she says, giving me a big hug. "How you holding up?"

I shrug. "I don't know. Everything's weird right now."

She nods and gently touches my shoulder. She opens her mouth to say something but changes her mind and smiles warmly. "You hang in there. I think getting out of the house will do you both some good."

Jules tosses their rag into the cleaning supply bucket and makes a break for the front door.

"Come back here first," 'Lita calls from down the hall. "Jules and Malika. Come here."

Jules turns to me. "She's using your first name. Must be serious."

Miss Celia raises her brows and runs her hand through her hair. "Better see what she wants before you go. She's been in a funny mood lately. I guess we all have."

"Come on," says Jules, grabbing my hand and leading me down the hall.

Jules's house is a lot like mine on the inside except 'Lita has her bedroom on the ground floor. I've only been in there once or twice in my whole life but she's calling us in there now and I can't help but feel a little nervous.

'Lita is sitting in a big uncomfortable-looking chair by an overstuffed bookcase. Her bed is neatly made and her room is decorated with all kinds of pictures and artwork. There's almost no free space on any of the four walls. The top of her dresser is crowded with small framed photographs and little decorative boxes. Hanging on the wall above her bed is the disguise she wore during her time as a Vanquisher. She was called the Mask of Red Death and wore a mask that looked exactly like a bloodred skull.

Jules follows my gaze. "'Lita, how do you sleep with that hanging over you? I'd be scared every time I looked up."

'Lita huffs and motions for us to come sit with her. There aren't any other chairs in her room so we sit on the rug at her feet and she leans toward us.

"I'm not afraid of anything." She reaches out and gently pulls a handful of Jules's hair through her fingers. "You're wearing your hair long, mi amor."

"You like it?" Jules asks.

'Lita smiles and runs her hand over the side of Jules's face. "If you like it, I love it." Jules rests their head on 'Lita's knee. "You're going out today?" 'Lita asks.

"Just for a little bit," Jules says.

"What are you taking with you?" 'Lita asks.

Me and Jules look at each other, confused.

"Just going out into the world unprepared?" asks 'Lita. "Seems foolish."

Jules tilts their head to the side. "What are we supposed to take?"

'Lita picks up a small wooden box with a flower carved on the top from the table next to her chair. She flips the lid open and pulls out three identical silver chains all about the length of a shoelace. "Pure silver. Very old. Put them on and give the other one to Cedrick. Don't take them off."

We do as we're told and I pocket the third chain to give to Ced. 'Lita reaches back inside her box and takes out a small photograph. It's torn and tattered around the edges. She turns it around to show us. The picture is a young woman with dark wavy hair and pale skin. She's smiling wide and in her hand is a glinting silver stake.

"Her name was Natalia," 'Lita says. "You probably know her better by her moniker, Nightside."

I can't keep my mouth from falling open. Another Vanquisher—an unmasked one. Jules's eyes grow wide.

"She was a tactician with a stake," 'Lita says. "She was strong and fast and knew her vampire lore better than anyone I'd ever come across. She was a fighter and she stood at my side for many years before the Reaping. We battled hordes of the undead together." She looks down at the picture, cradling it in her hands. "During the Reaping, she was killed by a fledgling vampire. She let her guard down for a split second and then she was gone."

I swallow hard. There's a monument to Nightside downtown in Travis Park and another one on the site of the last battle between the Vanquishers and the San Antonio hive, which took place at the park in the center of the city's Pearl district. The monument there marks the exact spot where Nightside perished.

"'Lita," Jules says. "Are you trying to scare us?"

"Yes," 'Lita answers sternly. "What we did that day cost us. We did not come out whole. We were broken and we lost so very much." Her eyes become glassy and she turns her face to the window. "Natalia was among the best of us and still, a monster cut her down in the prime of her young life. I don't care if we've eradicated every last vampire. We should still be cautious because as sure as I am that we did what we set out to do that day, there is always a doubt."

"That you didn't wipe them out?" I ask, stunned. The Mask of Red Death, someone who'd been at the Reaping, has a doubt?

'Lita only continues to stare out the window. "I pray that I am wrong. And every year that passes without incident makes me more secure in my belief that we have seen the last of them, but I will never take a chance. Especially when it comes to you." She turns back to us. "I miss Natalia every single day. But I see her in the two of you and in Cedrick. Your innocence, your confidence that things will go your way." She shakes her head. "I will stay vigilant and so will you." She says it like an order, like a command, like the leader of the Vanquishers would. "Now, go get some fresh air but be cautious and do not take unnecessary risks. Understand?"

"Yes, ma'am," Jules and I say in unison.

Me and Jules stand up and leave 'Lita's room as she places the photo of Nightside back in her box. Miss Celia meets us at the front door and opens it as we slip on our shoes and head out.

"We'll be back in a little while," Jules says.

"Be good," their mom says.

I wave at her but I catch something in her eyes before she ducks away. Something almost sad, just the way my parents had looked at me at the table this morning.

Jules closes the door behind us. "They keep talking to me like I'm going off to a war or something. 'You're so big. You're growing up so fast.' What's the deal?"

I shrug. "My parents are the same way. My mom said she's gonna try to let us go back to hanging out and stuff."

"My mom said the same thing. You think they talked?"

"I know they did," I say. "It's like they decided to be less strict when we kind of need them to be stricter. Especially after what we saw. And what's up with 'Lita showing us the picture? She never talks about that stuff."

"I know, right?" Jules says, sighing. "She keeps it all bottled up. Maybe it's just too much sometimes, you know?"

"Maybe," I say.

We go over to Cedrick's and before we get to the door he bursts out onto the porch, his shoes untied, his shirt half on. "Boog and Jules are here! Gotta go!"

He's pushing us toward our bikes when his dads come out onto the porch.

"Is your phone charged?" Mr. Alex asks.

"All of you need to stay together," says Mr. Ethan. "Don't talk to strangers!"

"What if they offer us candy?" Jules asks.

"Jules!" Cedrick yells. "Don't say that! We'll be right back in the house and I can't take it!"

"Kidding!" Jules calls.

"And I have my phone, too, Mr. Chambers," I say, holding it up.

Mr. Ethan smiles. "Because you're the responsible one, Boog."

"Love you, Ceddy," Mr. Alex calls.

"Oh my god, Dad! I thought we weren't gonna say Ceddy anymore. I'm twelve!"

"Sorry," Mr. Alex says, but I can see by his grin he's not sorry at all and it's hilarious.

Jules claps Cedrick on the back. "I like Ceddy. It's cute."

Cedrick rolls his eyes.

Mr. Alex waves. "Love you."

"Love you, too," Cedrick says.

We climb onto our bikes and pedal to the end of the block. We make the turn onto the cross street but only so that our families can't see us stop by the fence and huddle up.

"Did you get the book?" I ask Ced.

"Not yet. My dads have been on me like a fly on a hot turd all morning."

I slump over my handlebars. "Great. Well, maybe we start with visiting Aaron's mom."

"Are we still sure that's a good idea?" Jules asks. "What are we gonna say, exactly? Hi, Miss Kim, your son is an undead demon and he lives in the park now. So sorry!"

"He's not a demon," I say. But something occurs to me just then that gets me thinking. Every time we talk about the way the world was before the Reaping we hear about how monstrous vamps really were. They weren't cute or romantic like in the movies or in books. They were killers. They'd killed Nightside and a bunch of the Wrecking Crew. But I couldn't make that match up with what I saw when I looked at Aaron. Yes, he was changed in monstrous ways, but he was scared, and when I looked into his eyes I still saw him, he was still himself.

I shove my hands in my pockets and remember 'Lita's gift for Cedrick. I pull out the silver chain and hand it to him.

"What the heck is this?" he asks, taking it from me and holding it up in front of him.

"'Lita said we have to wear it at all times," I say. "It's silver. And she told us this really awful story about Nightside so maybe just do it to make her feel better."

"She told y'all a Vanquisher story and you didn't call me over?" He shoves the chain in his pocket. "I thought we were friends."

"Trust me, you didn't want to hear it," says Jules. "Hearing that story and seeing the mask on the wall was too much."

"She let you go in her room?" Cedrick looks back and forth between us. "I'm so mad at y'all. You saw the mask up close?" He tilts his head back and closes his eyes. "Y'all don't even love me at all. I know it."

"You're so dramatic," I say. "We love you, okay? We didn't know she was gonna take us in there like that. Can we talk about this later, though? Right now, I think we should talk to Aaron's mom to check in on her. Maybe we don't say anything about Aaron right now but we can at least say hi."

Cedrick is still salty but we all agree, hop off our bikes, and walk up to Aaron's front door. I ring the bell. His mom answers a moment later and I have to bite the inside of my cheek to keep my mouth from falling open when I catch sight of her. She has her hair tucked under a wrap but her edges are sticking out all around her face. The bags under her eyes are dark, the whites of her eyes bloodshot. She's been crying.

"Oh, Miss Kim," I say. "We're sorry to bother you. We just—"

"You're not bothering me at all. Come in," she says quietly.

We follow her into the living room where there are maps of San Antonio with grids drawn across them spread on a folding table. Stacks of missing posters with Aaron's smiling face sit in heaps on the floor. Half-empty cups of coffee are scattered around and empty takeout containers teeter on top of a too-full trash can.

"Excuse the mess," she says as she slumps into a chair. She rubs her temple like she has a headache. The angles of her face are sharper than I remember. "I don't have the energy to keep anything clean right now."

We sit on the couch and exchange glances. I don't know what I'm supposed to say.

"We would've come over sooner," I start. "But our parents have had us in the house this whole time."

Miss Kim nods. "They've been by. I can't thank them enough for all their help. They've been out searching when everybody else has given up." She readjusts herself in the chair. "They are right to keep a close eye on you. We always think something like this can't happen but here we are and I feel like I'm stuck in some kind of nightmare."

"I'm so sorry, Miss Kim," Cedrick says.

"Can we do anything for you?" Jules asks.

Miss Kim seems to fold in on herself. "Just don't forget about him—about Aaron."

A knot grows in my throat. Her sadness is like a heavy blanket. I can almost feel it wrapping itself around me.

"We could never do that," I say. "Never."

She smiles. "You know, I'm a scientist. I study viruses. With an illness you can try to prepare, you can try to accept how it might end. But this—this is like torture." She's crying now, tears carving little trails down her cheeks. "I don't know where he is or if he's hurt or scared." She sobs uncontrollably and her body rocks back and forth with each heave.

I get up and slide into the seat next to her. She puts her arms around me and I hug her tight, biting back my own tears.

"And I think the stress of it is doing something to my mind," she says, her face on my shoulder.

"What do you mean?" I ask.

She laughs a little, a hollow sound with no real feeling behind it. It's like that part of a person that makes them light up on the inside is gone. "I don't sleep. I can't. So, I was sitting in the front room, just sitting there doing nothing and I glanced at the back door. Through the glass I thought I saw—"

My heartbeat ticks up. Jules slides to the edge of the couch and Cedrick starts to play with a little string that has come loose from the seam of his jeans.

"I thought I saw him standing there," Miss Kim says. "Can you believe that? But if he was there, he would've come in. He would've told me he was okay. My mind was playing tricks on me. Showing me what I wanted to see."

I don't know what to say. A part of me wants to tell her what I know. But what is that exactly? That Aaron is a vampire? Maybe it'll make her feel better that he's not completely gone but he's also not the same as he was before. Is that something she can live with? Will she even believe me? I lean toward her and Cedrick clears his throat louder than he needs to.

When I glance at him, he shakes his head just a little as if he can tell that I'm weighing my options.

"I don't want to keep you, you all are clearly on your way to hang out," says Miss Kim. "And I know you've been cooped up." She stands up and ushers us toward the door. "Get out in the sunshine and have fun but be safe, okay?"

I give her another hug on our way out and she closes the door. We shuffle down the walkway and pick up our bikes.

"It makes my heart hurt," Jules says. "Seeing her like that. She's miserable."

"I wanted to tell her what we saw," I say.

"We can't," Cedrick says. "Not until we have more information. What if we're wrong? I mean, I'm pretty sure we're not, but I don't know. None of us have ever seen a real vamp. And what if we tell her and then something happens to her? Like, I'm pretty sure whatever creature bit Aaron does not want us spreading their business around."

"We need that book, Ceddy," I say.

The corners of Cedrick's mouth turn down. "I know."

"Do you know what it's called?" Jules asks. "Maybe we can find it at the library."

Cedrick shakes his head. "No, but I don't think it's the kind of book they have at the library. I'm telling you, the books were old. As soon as my parents go to sleep later, I can get it."

We agree to wait for Ced to get the book before we say anything to Aaron's mom or our own parents.

I pedal as fast as I can down the sidewalk with Cedrick and Jules racing behind me. I let the wind whip my face and I let the hot almost-summertime air fill my lungs. It feels good to be out in the open air after being stuck in the house but nothing is going to get me far enough away from the truth of what happened to Aaron. He should be with us, pedaling along the sidewalk, laughing with us, coming back to my house for movies and pizza. Even if I tell his mom what happened, things can never be the same as they were before. We can't ever have that back. I grip my handlebars and pump my legs as hard as I can, trying, and failing, to run away from how angry that makes me. We make our way to the Green and sprawl out in the grass right behind my house.

"Your dad got the fence fixed so fast," Cedrick says.

"I know," I say. "Him and some of his friends finished it this morning. He chopped up that whole tree. You saw that tarp in the garage and all that sawdust? It's completely gone."

"They didn't waste no time, huh?" Jules asks.

I think for a moment. "Do y'all know what three nines fine means?"

"Huh?" Jules asks.

"When my dad was on the phone the other day he said he needed something called three nines fine."

"You Google it?" Jules asks.

I nod. "Yeah but the only thing I found was a barbershop in Fresno, California."

Cedrick rolls up onto his elbow. "Was he talking about the fence when he said it?"

"Yeah. Do you know what he meant?"

"It's silver," says Ced.

Me and Jules both stare at him.

"It's like really, really good silver."

"But the fence is made of wood," I say.

Cedrick thinks for a minute, looking back and forth between the fence and us. "So you know how the Vanquishers had weapons? Threshold had silver stakes. Sailor's Knot had the rope with the silver threads."

"We know all that," says Jules.

"Let me finish," Cedrick says. "Carmilla had the crossbow. It shot silver stakes but there are witnesses, people who were at the Reaping, who said she stabbed a vamp with the bow itself."

"So?" I ask.

Cedrick widens his eyes like his point should be obvious.

"The bow was made of wood but it had silver inside it." He looks down at the ground. "That's what people say, anyway. And if your dad was tryna get his hands on some silver . . ." He glances at the fence.

I scramble to my feet and run my hands along the pickets. The ones facing the Green are wider than the ones between me and Ced's yard and they're splintered from years in the scorching Texas sun. They didn't take any damage when the storm hit so my dad didn't replace them. There's a narrow split in one of the boards near the base.

Jules and Cedrick come over and crouch down beside me as I gently tug at the piece of wood until it breaks off in my hand. I peer inside the small hole it left and to my amazement, there is something gleaming and glinting inside. I quickly grab my phone and turn on the flashlight, pointing the beam of light into the empty space.

"It's silver," I say.

We sit back in the grass in stunned silence. The fence pickets have silver cores. I can't see inside all the other ones but I'm sure it's the same thing and it sounds like my dad was making sure he had high-quality silver embedded in the new fencing, too.

"Why is it like that?" Jules asks.

I know my parents are protective but this is way beyond locking up or making sure we are all inside before sunset. I think of the posts jutting up out of the ground in front of the strip mall. The only reason they are there was because of what the site used to be—a medical facility. That extra layer of security was to keep vamps away but we don't need this kind of protection around our house in our boring neighborhood at the end of our boring street. At least that's what I thought before. Now, with what's happening to Aaron, well—things are different.

My phone buzzes in my hand.

MOM: Time to pack it in, baby. Ced and Jules need to head home too.

I turn my phone around and show them the message.

"See y'all tomorrow?" I ask.

We agree to meet up first thing in the morning and head home as the afternoon heat dials up to scorching.

Later that night, I lie in bed, waiting for my parents to go to their room. The curtains are open and I stare out my window watching the sky go from soft purple to pitch black, hoping to hear the sharp ping of gravel on the glass. I fall asleep while I'm waiting and wake up in the early morning hours like I'm falling, startling myself awake. My phone says it's four a.m. and I roll out of bed and go to my window.

I look down into the yard. Some of the grass is still torn up from where the tree fell. The fence is fixed and there's a single light on somewhere in the back of Cedrick's house but I can't tell which room it's coming from.

I'm just about to go back to bed, worried that something—or something else—has happened to Aaron when I spot him. He's standing out in the Green, behind the rear fence. He waves. I wave back, my heart leaping into a gallop. I motion for him to come closer but he shakes his head and puts his hands up. Something's wrong. He can't get in the yard. I stare at the pickets and remember what we'd found inside them. Silver. And if Aaron is a vampire, that means he won't be able to get anywhere close to my house. I mouth the words *stay there*. He nods. He might not be able to come in but I can at least try and meet him at the fence.

I turn and open my bedroom door and run right into my dad.

"Everything okay?" He peers into my room like he's expecting to see someone there. "I was just coming to check on you."

"I'm fine," I say. "I gotta pee."

"Oh, okay." He walks into my room, straight to the window, and my heart almost flips right out of my chest. He stares outside and then turns back to me. "We should keep these curtains closed, Boog. At least at night."

I try not to let him see me screaming internally. "Okay, Dad."

He gives me a hug and I go to the bathroom and pretend to use it, splashing around in the sink while I think of a way to get downstairs now that my dad's wandering the halls. I cut off the water and listen at the door. I don't hear anything but just in case, I walk back into my room, making sure my parents can hear me.

I go to the window again. Aaron is out there, but he couldn't have been when my dad was looking or he would have freaked out. He's holding something in his hand. It's too dark to see it clearly but it looks like a piece of paper. He walks up to the fence and extends his arm, pressing his palm against the side of the fence. He quickly draws it back as a puff of dark smoke rises into the air. He points to the fence. I don't understand, but when I blink, he's gone again.

CHAPTER 15

In the morning I pretend I left something out in the Green and slip through the back gate to see what Aaron was doing the night before. Stuck to the fence is a folded piece of paper. A note, from Aaron:

> Meet me at Helotes Park on Friday night. Right after sunset.

I fold it in half and shove it in my pocket, then text Jules and Cedrick to come over as soon as they can.

CEDRICK: I'll be over at 4. I GOT THE BOOK!

JULES: I'll be over ASAP

Late in the afternoon we huddle up in my basement, looking at the note Aaron left on the fence.

"Are we going?" Jules asks.

I hold the little scrap of paper in my hand. The edges are singed. I remember the smoke that billowed out of him as he tried to cross the threshold into my house—the same kind of smoke that had risen from his hand as he placed the note on the fence.

"We have to go," I say. "If he wants to meet us maybe he wants to tell us something. He couldn't get into the yard. I think because of the silver in the fence."

"How'd he get in before?" Cedrick asks.

I think for a minute. He'd been fully in the yard the night I opened the back door for him. It took me a minute to put it all together in my head. "The tree knocked down the fence. It was busted open enough for him to come through."

We all sit in silence for a moment. Every new thing we learn just confirms the terrible truth of what Aaron has become. It makes my heart ache. I can't think of a way back from this and the thought of losing Aaron makes me want to cry.

Cedrick slides a dusty old book onto the table. "Maybe this can help us figure out what to do now. Y'all are not gonna believe what I had to do to get it. I think my dads sleep in shifts. One of them is always awake and it's annoying so I only had, like, five minutes to grab this when they were both busy. I almost got caught."

"Do you think they'll notice it's missing?" I ask.

"Probably not," Cedrick says. "It's small. And there's, like, twelve other books on the same shelf that look just like it. I think they're part of a set."

I run my hand over the cover. It's smooth, like a thousand people have held it. The letters on the cover are so faded I can only make out a capital V pressed into it and the last little flecks of silver still clinging to the impression. I gently flip to the first page. It's handwritten in a fancy script.

"Does anybody even use cursive anymore?" Cedrick asks.

I squint at the lettering, trying to make it out. "It says, 'For those who fight in the shadows. For the Vanquishers.'"

"It's like a Vanquishers' handbook?" Jules asks. "Cool!"

"Shhhhh!" I shush them. "We cannot let anybody know we have this or we'll be on punishment forever. Then when we die we'll be ghosts and we'll still be on punishment."

"I'd like to know how that's gonna work," Cedrick says, trying his best to sound like he's not worried.

We lean close to the book and I whisper a few sentences aloud.

"The vampire's weaknesses are few and so obscure as to be nearly useless to the uninitiated. They can be trapped or held at bay by consecrated ground. The uninvited shall not pass a threshold, which can keep them out of certain spaces as long as the inhabitants are vigilant. Stakes of holly wood can destroy them but silver and prolonged exposure to daylight are most effective. The destruction of the maker can also reverse the change if performed soon after the initial bite but this is rarely accomplished. They are insidious, bewitching—the deadliest predator to ever roam these lands or any other. They are the undead—vampire."

Whoever wrote this had seen these creatures up close and knew things about them that only someone who had fought— and slain—them would have known. I grip the book tight as I try to keep my hands from trembling.

I turn the pages and come to a chapter halfway through that catches my attention. I read it aloud again. "The bite is its weapon and there are various outcomes, the most prominent being death. On rare occasions the wounds inflicted by the vampire heal, leaving the victim unchanged. In the rarest of circumstances, the bite causes a turning. Turning a human into a vampire is the least likely outcome of an interaction with the undead. It is a slow, agonizing transformation."

I put the book down and gently close the tattered cover. "That's what's happening to Aaron. He's turning. And from what we saw, he's pretty close to being a full-fledged vamp."

Jules sniffs as tears fill their eyes. "And it's hurting him and he's all alone out there. Boog, do you think he'll still be himself when he's fully changed? Is that even possible?"

I swallow the knot in my throat and put my arm around Jules. "I don't know."

Cedrick glances up at me. "This is real," he says. "What Aaron said—somebody bit him. Now he's turning. This is happening right now, right here."

"It's true. I know it. My gut is telling me it is," I say. "I was so scared of him, like I could feel it in my bones but . . ." I turn to Jules. "He's still himself. He's not a monster like it says in the books." I shove the dusty old book away from me. "He's scared and I'm not going to turn my back on him."

Jules wraps their arms around their waist and sits down on the floor. "What do we do?"

"If we're going to help Aaron we have to find out who bit him," I say. "It says right here in the book that if we can destroy his maker, we can change him back."

"If we can even get to the vampire who bit him fast enough," Jules says. "We don't have a single clue who it is."

"Does it say anything about how to recognize a vampire?" I ask. "I mean, we already know some of the rules, right? No reflection, can't come in unless they're invited, they hate garlic, and silver is deadly." I look down at the text again. "But this right here says 'prolonged exposure to daylight.' So they can be out in the sun for at least a little bit of time? I didn't know that. I thought it was just . . . poof! Dead as soon as the sun hits them."

Cedrick huffs. "We don't know as much as we think we do about vampires."

"If they can be out in the daytime, even for a little while, that changes things," says Jules. "It could be anybody."

Cedrick runs his hands over the top of his head. "Do they sparkle, like that man in that movie—what's it called—*Midnight*?"

"*Starlight*," Jules corrects.

"*Twilight*," I say. "And Aaron didn't look sparkly. He looked dead."

"Okay," Jules says, standing up. "Gimme that." They take the book and thumb through. "Open up a note on your phone and I'll tell you what to write."

I type as they flip through, reading out different bits of information that I enter into my phone.

"A stake made of holly can kill them but it has to be from a holly tree grown in consecrated ground. Garlic repels them." They turn a few more pages. "Vampires are allergic to silver the way some people are allergic to bee stings and direct contact with it causes an immediate and severe reaction." Jules sighs. "We know this stuff already. They don't have reflections. They have to be invited into your house. They can't just walk in."

I think back to the night Aaron was in the yard. I'd expected him to follow me into the house but he didn't—he couldn't.

"They are sensitive to sun," Jules continues reading. "This part says it's like fire on their skin but might not affect a fully matured vampire unless they're exposed to it for hours, maybe even days." They glance up at me. "So they *can* just walk around in the daylight?"

"That makes sense, right?" I say. "Aaron has just begun to change." I still can't believe I'm saying this about him. "That's why he's sensitive to the light. Whoever we're looking for could be able to walk around in the sunshine."

We all exchange worried glances and Jules closes the book.

"Okay," I say. "So let's think about this. We need to find the vampire who bit Aaron and we can use the stuff we found in that book and the stuff we already know to test any suspects."

"Suspects?" Cedrick asks. "We have suspects?"

"I mean Mr. Rupert is at the top of my list," I say. He's the only one on the list, actually. The only person who has been acting like a complete weirdo lately.

"So where do we get a stake made of holly?" Cedrick asks. "And do we have to stab them in the heart?"

I stare at Cedrick. "Umm, that's not really a test. What happens if we stake somebody and they aren't even a vampire?"

Cedrick presses his mouth into a tight line. "You right. You right."

"Let's try something that's not gonna get somebody dead, okay?" I ask. "And if we're careful, we can do it without them knowing and when we find out who it really is, then—"

"Then we stake them through the heart," Cedrick says.

Jules huffs loudly. "Imma have to keep my eye on you because you sound like a whole killer right now."

"Let's start with mirrors," I say. "Vampires don't have reflections, right? So we bring a mirror, something small, maybe see if we can catch somebody that way?"

"And garlic," Jules says. "That'll be easy to get. We have a bunch in the kitchen."

"So do we," I say.

"Do we have silver?" Cedrick asks.

The silver chain 'Lita had given me is looped around my wrist and I run my fingers over it. "We have these. Maybe we just wear them around our necks or something. And because we don't really have any suspects other than Mr. Rupert, I say we just test everybody."

"Everybody?" Cedrick asks. "In the whole school? That's a lot of people."

"Then we should get started tomorrow. First thing in the morning."

CHAPTER 16

I slip exactly seven bulbs of garlic into my backpack the next morning. I could probably take a hundred out of the trash can–sized bin my mom keeps them in before she'd notice but seven seems like a good number for now. Jules is waiting on their bike when I come out of the house. Their backpack looks bulkier than usual.

"I got three mirrors and some spray bottles," they say.

"What do we need spray bottles for?" I ask as Cedrick meets us on the sidewalk.

"We can crush up the garlic and put it in there with some water. We can just mist people in the hallway." They look at me like I should understand that this is the best plan ever. "I mean, were we just gonna hand people a clove of garlic and see if their hand falls off?"

"Do you think that's what's gonna happen?" Cedrick asks. "Don't judge me but I kind of hope so."

"See?" says Jules. They point to Cedrick. "I'm watching you, sir."

I think for a minute. "I actually don't know what's gonna happen so we should be prepared for anything."

"I have the book in my bag," Cedrick says. "Maybe there's something else in there. But look at this." He takes out his phone and points the screen toward me. He swipes through a bunch of pictures of trees, just like the ones in my yard, like the one that fell down during the storm. "They're holly trees."

"For real?" I ask. "We have vampire killing trees in our yard?"

"Are there any pieces of that one that came down in the storm?" Jules asks. "Maybe we can use that for something?"

I shake my head but then I remember that my dad saved a piece to make my mom a table. "Hang on," I say. Slipping off my bike I go to the garage to see if the stump is still there under the blue tarp I'd seen a few days ago. I twist the handle and it doesn't turn but the door swings open. I examine the doorknob. It's a simple twist lock and it looks like my mom or dad probably meant to lock the door on the way out but it didn't close all the way.

Sawdust still covers the floor and the blue tarp is covering the table my dad is supposed to be working on but it looks different, like it's closer to the floor than it had been a few days earlier and the tarp has been readjusted.

I grab the edge and yank it up, expecting to find the world's ugliest table but instead I find a pile of neatly carved wooden stakes. My heart thuds in my chest and I quickly look around. I feel like I'm seeing something that is supposed to be a secret.

I crouch and pick up one of the stakes. It's about the size of a ruler and the end is so sharp I'm positive it'll cut me if I touch it. I held a replica stake on a field trip to the Vanquisher museum when I was in the third grade. It was made of plastic and weighed almost nothing. This thing isn't like that. It's solid, heavy as a brick. I turn it over in my hand and find a small hole on the flat end. The garage light glints off something inside it—silver.

Footsteps behind me send me scrambling to recover the pile of stakes but it's just Jules and Cedrick.

"You good?" Cedrick asks, but as his gaze lands on the stake in my hand he goes silent.

Jules rushes up to me. "What are you doing? Where did you get that?"

I point to the tarp. "There's a whole pile of them under there. And they have silver cores."

I hand the stake to Cedrick and pull the tarp away to show them what I'd found.

"What is going on?" Jules asks.

"I—I don't know." My parents have to know this is here.

But why? What do they need these for? I take the stake back from Cedrick and shove it in my bag. "We gotta get out of here."

I nudge Jules and Cedrick out the door and pull it all the way closed, making sure it's locked. I climb on my bike.

"Boog, what are your parents doing with those stakes?" Cedrick asks.

"Look what else they've been doing," I say quietly. "The fence, the dirt. They know something is going on."

"How?" Cedrick asks.

"Maybe they're just being overly careful," Jules offers.

"I really don't know but we keep it to ourselves for now, okay? Focus on our plan. Find out who bit Aaron and then we'll figure out why they have those things." I motion toward the garage. My parents are hiding something from me. They want me to be honest with them about everything, they want me to trust them, but they're lying to me. They have to know something's up.

I pedal away from the house with a million thoughts tumbling through my head, but I decide to take my own advice and put my mind on helping Aaron.

When we get to school, we sneak into the bathroom by the gym that nobody ever uses and fill our spray bottles with crushed-up garlic and water.

"This smells like the stuff we use to clean the house," says Jules.

I nod. That's what we should be using but if I'd asked my

mom to make us a batch, we'd have given ourselves away. So instead, we're here in the bathroom that permanently smells like boo boo, crushing up garlic and filling our spray bottles. If anybody walks in on us there's not going to be a way to explain what we're doing. So we work fast and clean up as much of our mess as possible, flushing garlic skins down the toilet and wiping up water that has splashed on the mirrors and floor.

Armed with spray bottles, a dusty old Vanquisher guidebook, and all the rumors about vampires we've ever heard, we start our test of the student body at Victor Garcia Middle School.

CHAPTER 17

That morning I spray Kayla Carlisle and Mallory James as we're dressing out for PE. I try not to make it obvious but Kayla catches sight of my spray bottle.

She scrunches up her nose "What is that?"

"Body spray," I say.

"Body spray is supposed to smell good," Mallory says angrily.

Neither of them have a reaction, even though I'm not sure what a reaction would even look like. Will they burst into flames? Will they shrivel up and turn to dust?

"Smells good to me," I say before slipping out into the gym.

Tuesday afternoon, I meet Jules and Cedrick after PE and Cedrick hands me his phone with an ugly picture of him and three dudes from Mr. Baker's eighth grade class. They're all smiling except Cedrick, who looks like the flash caught him midsneeze.

"Yikes," I say.

"It's none of them because they all showed up in the picture," Cedrick says, clear tone of disappointment in his voice. "Then I caught Hailey and her entire soccer team in the hall. You know how they get when they're hyped up after practice—high-fiving and stuff. I jumped in."

"What?" Jules asks, biting back a smile. "You joined in the team's celebration?"

Cedrick is grinning so hard I can see all his teeth. "Yup. They didn't care. And look." He holds up his hand. The silver chain from 'Lita is wrapped around his palm. "I think it touched every single one of them. No smoke, no flames. Nothing."

By Friday morning we've tested fifty-six students and two teachers and so far have only managed to get on everyone's nerves. If only they knew what we know, maybe they'd understand.

"There are way too many people in this school to just test everybody," Jules says.

They're right. This is taking too long and some part of me feels like we're running out of time. We have to find a way to narrow things down. "It's gotta be somebody we know was at the rink that night. Can you name anybody you saw?"

"I saw Jared and his friends from seventh grade," Jules says. "I definitely saw Elijah. But see, that's what I'm talking about.

That's, like, six people and there had to be two hundred people at the rink that night."

"Has anybody been acting weird since then?" I ask.

Jules pulls at their braid. "Not that I can think of. But what does that mean anyway? Are we looking for people acting weird or acting like vampires?"

"What does it look like when you act like a vampire?" Cedrick asks. "Are we thinking that people are gonna be hanging upside down from the ceiling? Suckin' on neck bones in the hallway? What?"

"No," Jules says angrily. "But c'mon. No way a vampire is here in the school every day and acting completely normal."

"Maybe not," I say. "But if it's nothing obvious, then how do we narrow it down?"

None of us have an answer and feeling defeated, we make our way to the lunchroom. We watch the other students, trying to see if anyone is exhibiting any vampirish behavior.

Cedrick rests his chin on his forearms as he picks at his food. "If somebody would just take a little nibble of somebody's neck, we'd have this whole thing solved right now."

Everyone is eating their lunches, people are laughing, joking around. Nothing unusual until—I catch a glimpse of Mr. Rupert's shiny bald head. He's leaned over, his eyebrows pushed together, talking to a short kid with hair so blond it's almost white.

"Look," I say.

They glance over just as Mr. Rupert disappears into the hallway and the kid takes a seat at a table, his back to us.

"We gotta slip him some garlic," I say. "We have to test Mr. Rupert."

The blond kid sits bolt upright and turns his head so that I can see the side of his face. I can't tell for sure, but I think he's smiling.

The bell rings and I grab my bag. The stake is still inside and I hope that I don't have to use it. Could I stake weird old Mr. Rupert? I think about it and the answer surprises me. Maybe.

Jules and Cedrick go to their classes but I hang out in the hall, taking my time as everyone else rushes off. Every time someone passes by, I wonder if they're the person responsible for what is happening to Aaron. Is there really a vampire roaming these halls? A little shiver runs up my back at the thought. The bell rings.

"Great," I say to myself. I'm tardy. Mom will love that.

Papers rustle somewhere in the hall and I turn to see the blond kid from the lunchroom trailing behind me.

"You're late for class," I say. My mom always tells me that people who are trying to be sneaky think they're great at it, but if you call them out, let them know that you see them trying to be slick, most of the time they'll just go away.

"So are you," says the kid. He doesn't even look up. Just fishes around in his bag.

I pick up the pace. Behind me, his footsteps pick up, too. I glance over my shoulder. He's still looking inside his bag. It could be my imagination or the fact that I'm already on edge but I swear this kid is matching my pace. I reach into my bag and my fingers brush the wooden stake. I take a deep breath. Let me not impale my classmate before I even know what's really going on. I grab the little spray bottle instead, stop dead in my tracks, and as I pivot around, spray him right in the face. He blinks repeatedly at me.

"What'd you do that for?" he asks angrily, wiping his face with his shirt. He blinks and some of the spray runs down his forehead directly into his eye. He rears back and lets out a high-pitched yelp.

I quickly duck into Mrs. Lambert's room and slam the door shut behind me.

"Malika?" Mrs. Lambert asks. She's eating lunch at her desk. She closes up her plastic container and walks over to me. "Everything okay?"

"Yeah—I just—I thought—" I don't know what to say. I thought a little blond boy was a vampire and that he was tryna get me so I doused him with garlic water?

She glances out the small window in the door. "Thought maybe Mr. Rupert was chasing you."

"Oh yeah?" I ask. I glance out the window and the kid is gone. I sigh. "So you see how weird Mr. Rupert is, right? It's not just me."

She nods. "He takes his job entirely too seriously."

"I thought I was the only one who noticed," I say. Mrs. Lambert has something black stuck between her teeth. I motion to it and she quickly covers her mouth.

"I'm so sorry." She laughs. "I had a meeting that ran over. I only have a few minutes to finish my lunch." She takes a swig from her water bottle and turns back to me. "So Mr. Rupert, huh?"

"Why is he so worried about what I'm doing all the time?"

She spots the spray bottle in my hand. "What is that?"

"Uh—nothing." I put the bottle back in my bag.

She sniffs at the air. "Is that—garlic?"

"How'd you know?" I bite the inside of my lip. I'm way too good at telling on myself.

"Malika, honey, you reek of it." She pinches her nose.

"So what do you think I should do about Mr. Rupert?" I ask, trying to change the subject.

"My advice? Ignore him. He thinks he's going to make a name for himself here—be the good guy that everybody comes to when they have a problem." She rolls her eyes. "His ego is out of control and he thinks he's better than the rest of us."

I start to laugh but as I look Mrs. Lambert over, she's got one fist balled up and she's tapping her foot on the tile. "I don't think I've ever seen you so irritated," I say.

She smiles warmly and a fly lands directly on the tip of her nose. She bats it away but as it buzzes off, I see that a half dozen more have gathered on Mrs. Lambert's Tupperware containers. She rushes over and swats them away.

"Ugh! I'm so sick of this," she says as she sweeps her containers into her desk drawer and grabs a flyswatter. "I'm pretty sure something crawled into one of the vents and died. These flies are all over the place." She sits back down at her desk and swats at the flies buzzing around her head.

"I gotta go," I say.

"See you Monday, Malika," she says. "Please let me know if Mr. Rupert gives you any more trouble."

I rush out, hurrying down the hall and into B building. There's no sign of the blond boy anywhere. Mr. Keller, my Vampire History teacher, doesn't seem to care that I'm late. He waves me in as he fumbles with the digital projector. I sit at the back of the class and take out Aaron's note. I can't wait to see him. I need to make sure he's okay—if that's even possible considering he's turning into a whole vampire now.

"Remember, cases like the Mercy Brown incident in Exeter were hushed up, written off as illness or superstition, but the truth was that vampires had found a new home where they could run unchecked with an endless supply of victims whose deaths were ignored, discounted, or in the most sinister of circumstances, welcomed."

"And what about Dracula?" one of the other students asks.

Mr. Keller rolls his eyes. "What about him, Kevin?"

"C'mon," Kevin whines. "I wanna hear something exciting."

A bunch of kids hoot and holler in agreement. Mr. Keller cuts off the projector and perches himself on the edge of his desk. "Dracula is a myth based on a real person."

Boos and stifled laughter erupt but Mr. Keller silences them with an angry glare.

"Tell me which part of anything that we've talked about seems funny to you." Mr. Keller stares Kevin in the face. "Vampires were monsters. They were not beautiful people in capes wandering the halls of a castle somewhere in Transylvania. They were flesh and blood and they were monstrous. It's a pity we've forgotten that. They were apex predators and their extinction should be looked at with the same sorrow that the extinction of any other species would. Imagine if the great white shark went extinct, or the tiger. It would be a loss for the natural world. And yet, we wiped vampires off the face of the earth and see it as something to celebrate." He shakes his head. "Shameful."

It's no secret that there are people, like Mr. Keller, who have an affinity for vampires. My dad almost got in a fight with a dude at Vanquisher Appreciation Week last year because the guy said he wished a vampire had bitten Carmilla. There are people out there who really wish vampires had defeated the Vanquishers.

The intercom crackles to life. "Mr. Keller?"

"Yes?" Mr. Keller asks, annoyed.

"Malika Wilson to the office for a moment please."

Mr. Keller looks back at me and gives me a quick nod. "She's on her way."

I gather my things and walk down to the office and check in at the desk. Mr. Hansen tells me to have a seat.

"Is something wrong?" I ask. "Am I in trouble?"

He crosses his arms over his chest. "Should you be?"

"No," I say.

"Then you should have nothing to worry about." He sniffs at the air the same way Mrs. Lambert had and leans as far away from me as his desk will allow. I shrink into the seat and avoid eye contact.

A few minutes tick by before I hear one of the doors open near the back of the office. Mr. Rupert comes out and when he sees me, his expression doesn't change at all. I can't tell if he's mad. His face always looks like that.

"Miss Wilson," he says. "Please come into my office."

From behind him, the blond boy from the hallway pokes his head out.

"Great," I mumble to myself. I'm definitely in trouble.

I follow Mr. Rupert into his office. His desk is way too big for the room and the chairs on the side closest to me are all crowded together. The blond boy is seated near the wall. Mrs. Lambert was right. Mr. Rupert takes this too seriously.

"Please have a seat," he says.

I sit and hold my bag on my lap.

"Preston says you sprayed some kind of foul-smelling substance in his face while he was walking in the hallway."

"He was following me," I say.

"I was not," Preston snaps. "I was late to class so I was tryna hurry up."

"I could feel you breathing on me." I glance over at him. "Did you have to be that close?"

Preston's face turns a shade of red I didn't know was possible on human skin.

"All right," Mr. Rupert says calmly. "Let's just take things down a notch. What did you spray him with and why?"

"It was water."

"Liar," says Preston. "It stinks!"

"Maybe it was your upper lip," I offer.

"Preston, would you please excuse us for a moment?" Mr. Rupert says with a pained look on his face.

Preston shoves his chair back and it bangs into the wall. He stomps out and sits in a chair right in front of the office window.

Mr. Rupert leans forward in his chair, his fingers tented under his chin. "What was in the water, Miss Wilson?"

I take a deep breath. I could lie but I smell like I took a bath in the stuff so there's really no point. "Garlic."

He raises an eyebrow and for the first time since I met him, the corner of his mouth twitches—like he's gonna smile. It's horrifying.

"Do you still have the bottle?" he asks.

I nod.

He picks up a small metal trash can and tips it toward me. "Toss it."

I take out the spray bottle and for a moment, I think about spraying him.

"Now, Miss Wilson," he says.

I chuck it in and he sets the trash can back on the floor and nudges it away from him with his foot.

"Why are you carrying around a bottle of garlic-laced water?"

I look down. "It was just—an experiment. A test."

Mr. Rupert leans forward, his arms folded across his desk. "And what were you testing for, exactly?"

"It's nothing. It doesn't matter. I won't do it again."

"That's not really an answer, is it?"

"Can I ask *you* a question?" I decide to turn it around on him.

He sits back and then gives a little nod.

"Why are you so worried about what me and my friends are doing? You've been bothering us since you showed up."

His face is a mask of irritation again. "It's my job."

"You keep saying that but we've had other counselors," I say. "I can't even tell you their names because nobody ever talked to them and they definitely didn't come around introducing themselves or checking in on us at lunch or—"

"It sounds like you've had some very lackluster counselors," he says stiffly. "I do take my job quite seriously and I would appreciate it if you could respect that."

I press my lips together to keep from back talking him. My mom has a rule. I can and should stick up for myself, even with teachers, but I'm not allowed to be disrespectful if they haven't disrespected me first. What Mr. Rupert is doing is right on the border of rude and annoying so I just keep my mouth shut.

"I'm not sure what you're up to, or what you hope to accomplish by spraying your classmates with whatever is in that bottle but I'm going to ask you to stop." He narrows his eyes at me. "I'm *telling* you to stop."

I stare back at him. "Why?" I'm tempted to ask him if he's afraid he's going to get found out.

He raises an eyebrow and his mouth turns down. "Because you could hurt someone. Someone could be allergic."

"To garlic?"

"Deathly allergic," he says.

He draws out the word "deathly" as he stares at me and a shiver runs up my back. A bolt of fear shoots straight through me. I study his face. I can't really see his teeth when he talks so I can't tell is he's hiding fangs. His eyes are brown, not black with flecks of red like Aaron's. He doesn't look like a day-walking vampire but I'm still not 100 percent sure.

"You're dismissed, Miss Wilson," he says as he shuffles some papers around on his desk. "Try to stay out of trouble."

I grab my bag and leave. I shoot Preston an angry glance and he gives me a smug little smile.

My last class drags by and I all but run out of class and meet Cedrick and Jules at the bike rack.

"It's Mr. Rupert," I say.

"Come on, Boog," Jules says. "You don't know that."

"Aaron can't remember who it was," says Cedrick in a whisper. "He didn't get a clear look at them at all. It could be anybody."

I shake my head. "It's him. He called me to his office and I think he knows what I was trying to do with the garlic."

Jules's eyebrows shoot up. "Did he say that?"

"No, but—can't you just believe me?" I glance from Jules to Cedrick, feeling desperate.

"We believe you," Jules says. "We do. But how are we supposed to prove it and who are we gonna prove it to? Like once we find out. What are we gonna do?"

"We're gonna go meet Aaron and we're gonna make a plan," I say.

I know how it sounds. I understand how unlikely it is that Mr. Rupert could be one of the cursed undead, but every interaction I have with him makes one thing crystal clear—he's hiding something.

CHAPTER 18

I hop on my bike and we take the shortcut to my house. I drop off my stuff and tell my mom that we're going to go to the park down the block.

She glances out the window. "Be back at four thirty."

That's too early. Aaron won't be at the park until after the sun sets, which according to Google is at exactly six fifty-four. "Can I go to Cedrick's after?"

"Sure," she says. "Text me when you get there. Four thirty, Boog. Got it?"

"Yes, ma'am," I say. I go back outside and get on my bike.

"What are we doing?" Cedrick asks.

"Follow me," I say.

Jules and Cedrick follow me to the park. We lay our bikes in the grass and wait on a bench under a big willow tree, trying to stay out of the blistering afternoon sun.

"My mom wants me back at Cedrick's at four thirty," I say.

"How are we gonna stay out here till six?" Jules asks.

I lean back on the bench. "If we just stay here, they'll come looking for us." I look over at Cedrick. "Have you ever stayed out past curfew? Other than when we met Aaron?" Cedrick shakes his head. So does Jules. I haven't either. I'd never really had a reason to until now. "I'm staying. I need to talk to him."

Jules scoots close to me. "We're gonna be in so much trouble."

"I have an idea that could buy us some time but we'll be in even more trouble if we do it," I say.

Cedrick huffs. "Do you have any ideas that won't get us in trouble?"

"No," I say. At least I'm being honest. "Text your dad and ask him if you can come to my house. Don't let him tell you no."

"Yeah, sure. Just don't let him say no," Cedrick says sarcastically. He taps his temple. "Why didn't I think of that?"

"Beg him," I say. "Do that little whiny thing you do when you're trying to get your own way."

"You told your parents you were coming to my house," says Cedrick. "Now I'm telling them I'm going to yours?"

I nod. "Jules should do it too. That way nobody will be expecting us and when we go home we can just say we had an argument or something."

"Do you sit around and think of terrible plans?" Cedrick asks. "Because this one is special, Boog."

It might be a bad plan but Cedrick and Jules are already texting and soon everyone has a cover for where they're supposed to be.

We stay in the park—together—and wait for Aaron to show up.

"What if they find out we're not at each other's houses?" Jules asks. "How long before they're out looking for us."

"Not long," I say. I'm suddenly more nervous about my parents than I am about meeting my vampire friend in the park after the sun sets.

"Should we hide?" Cedrick asks, glancing around the park. "Just in case?"

"Good idea," says Jules.

We crowd behind the trunk of a large oak tree so that we can't be seen from the road. At six forty-five my phone buzzes. I glance at the screen.

MOM: CALL ME RIGHT NOW

Cedrick's and Jules's phones go off, too. My heart kicks up. I switch my phone to silent and turn off my location.

"We're so dead," Cedrick says.

"Yeah," Jules says. "Listen, caskets are expensive. Just bury me loose."

"Loose?" I ask.

"You know. Just dig a little hole and kick some dirt over me. No box. Nothin'."

I bust out laughing even though I've never been this scared

225

in my entire life. Getting attacked by a vampire almost sounds better than having to face my parents.

The sun dips low in the sky and as darkness pulls itself over us like a blanket, I spot Aaron walking up from the part of the park that leads to the trails that snake through the thick groves of trees. I jump up and run to him with Jules and Ced trailing cautiously behind me.

"Aaron!" I'm so happy to see him but I stop an arm's length away. He looks different from the last time I saw him. There are fewer red flecks in the blackness of his eyes. His movements are more fluid, like he's not quite touching the ground as he walks up. He looks me over and shrugs.

"Hey, Boog," he says with a little smile, and suddenly none of that other stuff matters. He's still Aaron. I give him a hug, ignoring the cold stiffness of his body. I don't want to think about it. He gently presses his hands against my back, like he's afraid I'm going to break.

"Thanks for meeting me," he says quietly. He still looks so afraid and it breaks my heart. "I couldn't get back into your yard."

"It's the fence," I say. "It has silver inside. My dad set it up like that."

"Oh," he says. "Please tell me you had some luck finding out who bit me?"

Me and Jules exchange glances.

"Not really," Cedrick says. "It's a lot harder than we thought it was gonna be."

"But we'll keep trying," I say quickly. "We'll find whoever it is. We do have some ideas but we need a little more time."

Aaron's mouth turns down and he grips his hands together in front of him. "It's okay. I know it's a lot to ask and it could be dangerous for you so maybe you shouldn't do it at all."

I put my hand on his arm. "Don't give up on us yet. We're gonna keep looking. We might need to think of some other ways to do it because going around the school spraying people with garlic water is drawing way too much attention."

His thick eyebrows push up over his strangely dark eyes. "Is that what y'all were doing?"

Jules tugs on their ponytail. "Yeah. We've tried the garlic spray, some silver, pictures, mirrors. You name it, we tried it."

"We saw your mom," I say. "She told us she saw you outside the back door. She thinks she's losing her mind. She's trying to prepare herself for the worst." I pause, thinking of what the "worst" actually is. Maybe his mom thinks hearing that her son is dead is the worst thing she can think of but I can guarantee that she hasn't thought of the possibility that Aaron has been turned into a vampire. Is that worse? I just don't know.

Aaron looks down at the ground. "I miss her so much. I went to the house thinking I could just tell her everything but I'm so scared she's gonna be afraid of me. How can I tell her what happened?" he asks. "How can I make her understand?"

"She loves you," Jules says. "She'll understand. We might have to think of a good way to break it to her, though."

Aaron nods. "I don't know who did this to me and I'm afraid that if I go home, they'll come after her."

"We're worried about that, too," I say. "Now that we know what's happening to you, maybe the vampire that bit you will want to shut us up."

Jules grips the sleeve of my shirt.

"I didn't really think of that," says Aaron, his voice like a hollow whisper. "I'm so sorry. I don't want anything to happen to any of you." Aaron is suddenly standing by the bench. He moves so fast it's like he disappears, then reappears in one blink.

Cedrick swallows a yelp.

"Sorry," Aaron says. "I can't control what's happening to me." He stretches his hands out in front of him, opening and closing them. "I feel like everything is different."

"Yeah, well, you're a vampire now," says Cedrick.

Jules huffs. "Thanks for stating the obvious, Ceddy."

Cedrick digs the tip of his shoe into the grass and stares down at the ground. "I mean, it's true."

I walk over to Aaron and take his hand. "You're still you. Maybe some things are different but, so? People change all the time."

"Do they grow teeth like this?" Aaron opens his mouth wide. His canines are elongated and razor sharp. They're curved just a little, like a snake's fangs. His jaw sits open unnaturally, like it can come apart at the hinge. He closes it and breathes deep. "Is that the kind of change you're talking about?"

"Maybe," Cedrick cuts in. He's doing a really bad job of pretending like he's not scared. I can see him calculating how fast he can book it to his bike but he stays put. "There's a kid in Mr. Lee's class who has an extra set of molars."

"That's not the same thing at all," says Jules, clearly annoyed.

"I know," says Cedrick. "I'm just sayin'. People have weird teeth sometimes."

I can't keep from grinning. Cedrick trying to make Aaron feel better for being a vamp is sweet.

"Do they crave blood?" Aaron asks. "Do they—" He stops short.

He's holding something back. I can't even imagine what other changes he's been going through.

"You gotta go see your mom," I say. The more I think about it the more I feel like we need to tell someone what's happening and Miss Kim is probably our best bet. We're in way over our heads.

Suddenly there's a high-pitched squeal of tires skidding across the road. A rush of air blasts my face and the top of the oak tree we're standing under rustles like something has shot straight through its branches. Aaron is gone and my parents along with Miss Celia and Cedrick's dad are piling out of my dad's SUV.

My mom comes barreling out and rushes up to me. Her face damp, her eyes red. "Get in the car. Now."

Jules and Cedrick hurry past her and Miss Celia puts her hand over her heart and takes a long deep breath. I start to follow them but my mom steps in front of me.

"What are you thinking?" she asks, her voice tight. The disappointment in her tone is the worst part. She reaches up and runs her hands over my face, down the sides of my neck, then exhales slowly. My dad stands next to her but he's not looking at me. He's scanning the park behind me.

"Mom, I—"

"I don't wanna hear it," she says through gritted teeth, her face a mask of anger and relief and sadness. "Do you know how dangerous it is to be out here? Your friend disappeared. Did you even think about that?"

I want to say no because I know what happened to Aaron and he isn't missing, but I'm not bold enough to do that. I know I'm in the wrong but I had to meet him.

She steers me back to the car and I get in next to Jules and Cedrick. Miss Celia and Cedrick's dad sit in the third-row seats. We pull off and head toward home. Cedrick's dad looks out the rear window the entire time. Nobody says a single word.

CHAPTER 19

No phone. No TV. No bikes. No guests. Being on punishment is always bad but this is the worst it's ever been. My mom barely speaks to me the entire next day. My dad tells me it'll be okay. He's mad, too, but with my mom it's something else. I messed up. I know that and even I agree that I should be on punishment for a little while.

I can't call or text Cedrick or Jules at all. I do catch Cedrick in his bedroom window and we write on notebook paper and hold it up. His note says, "How long?" I think he's asking if my parents have said how long I'll be grounded. They haven't, so I write back "4 ever I think." He writes back "Same." To see Jules's window I'd have to go into my parents' room and that's not happening so I have to wait until we're at school on Monday to talk.

At the lunch table we sit in our usual spot.

Jules rests their head on their outstretched arms. "This is the worst. I've never seen my mom so mad. Ever. And 'Lita. Oh my god, you guys, she's even worse."

Cedrick picks at his burrito. "My dads, too. I don't know what to do. They haven't even said when I'm gonna be ungrounded."

"My mom did," says Jules. "She said I'll be grounded the rest of my natural-born life. So what? Like, ninety more years? No big deal."

"Why the long faces?" Mr. Rupert appears at our table like the bugaboo he is.

Cedrick jumps and almost chokes on a bite of his burrito. Jules slaps him hard on the back and the little chewed-up piece of tortilla shoots out and smacks against the table.

Mr. Rupert turns to me. "Miss Wilson, your mother has asked me to remind you that she will be waiting outside and that you are not to step one foot off this campus unless you are in her company."

"She called you?" I ask.

"My number is listed," Mr. Rupert says stiffly. "Parents and guardians are allowed to contact me at their leisure."

"Right," I say. "I wasn't planning on going anywhere I'm not supposed to."

"So you've had a change of heart from the other night?"

I stare up at Mr. Rupert. "She told you about that?"

"She did." He looks at Cedrick, then Jules, then me again. "I told her that if she needed me to remind you that your friend Aaron is still missing—"

"I know!" I shove my tray away and stand up. I look past Mr. Rupert. "See y'all later."

I storm out of the lunchroom and go to the restroom where I sit in the stall and try to get myself together. Now my mom is having Mr. Rupert check in on me? She doesn't even understand how much of a creep he is and that he's at the top of my list of people who might know what happened to Aaron. I feel like I don't know what to do anymore. Tears sting my eyes as I stare up at the ceiling.

The main door to the bathroom creaks open and someone else walks in. I wait for them to go into one of the other stalls so I can go out without anyone noticing that I was crying on the toilet. That's the last thing I need people starting rumors about.

I don't hear any footsteps and nobody walks past the stall. I decide I'll just make a break for it but as soon as I open the door I run directly into Mrs. Lambert.

"Oh! Malika, I'm sorry, I thought this bathroom would be empty." She chucks a stack of plastic containers in the trash can and as she does one of the lids pops off. A dozen flies escape from inside and start buzzing around the trash can. "I forgot about these in my desk and now they're infested." She stares into the trash can. "Those were my favorite containers, too." She turns back to me and gives me the once-over. "You okay? You look a little upset."

I sigh. "Can I tell you something?"

"Of course." Her face softens and she leans toward me. "What's up?"

"I don't like Mr. Rupert. At all. He's always in my business and now my mom is asking him to keep an eye on me because I got in trouble at home."

"You already know how I feel about him. Stuffy old man needs to park his butt somewhere." She crosses her arms over her chest. "He's overstepping. And I don't like the stress it's putting on students like yourself."

I hesitate, thinking about everything that's happened over the past few weeks. About Aaron. About my parents' acting like a horde of vamps are going to descend on my house at any moment.

"Malika," Mrs. Lambert says gently. "What's on your mind? Anything I should worry about?"

For a second, I consider telling her everything. She's my favorite teacher and she's always so supportive of me but I have no idea where to start.

"It's—it's nothing. I just stayed out a little too late with my friends and got in huge trouble."

Her eyebrow shoots up. "You and the Squad up to no good?" She looks shocked. "I never took you for a rule breaker, Boog. At least not at home."

"I'm not. I mean, not really. It was just this once, and I won't do it again." That's probably true. I definitely don't think I'll ever have the chance to sneak out again anyways.

"Nobody's perfect," Mrs. Lambert says, giving my arm a squeeze. "Keep your head up. You're a smart girl. I'm sure everything will work out."

"Thanks, Mrs. Lambert." It feels nice to have her on my side.

I don't see Jules or Cedrick for the rest of the day. My dad is waiting in the truck when the bell rings and I climb into the passenger seat.

"How was your day?" he asks as we circle back to the house.

"Terrible," I say. "Did you know Mom is having Mr. Rupert keep an eye on me at school?"

He grimaces. "Of course."

I whip my head around. "Dad, come on. I stayed out a little past the time that Mom wanted me back. I didn't skip class or anything like that. Y'all are actin' like I killed somebody."

"First off, watch your tone," my dad says, his voice low and serious. "We will be respectful to each other if we're going to talk about this."

I sigh and nod my head.

He keeps his eyes on the road. "You didn't just stay out a little past the curfew your mom gave you. You, Jules, and Cedrick lied to us about where you would be. And on top of that, y'all stopped responding to texts and calls, and you were out after—" He stops and clears his throat.

"After what? After the streetlights came on?"

"Yes," he says. "You know how we feel about that. There were a bunch of things and that—along with Aaron's disappearance—made us extremely worried. We love you. All of you. Try to put yourself in our shoes. We couldn't get ahold of any of you. You think it's not serious but it is. More than you can imagine."

I look down into my lap. "I'm sorry, Dad. I really am."

He reaches over and puts his hand on my shoulder. "I know. It's okay. There are some consequences for what happened but you'll get back on track and everything will be okay."

When we pull up to my house there's a car in the driveway and my dad does a double take.

"You expecting someone?" I ask.

"No," he says.

He puts the car in the garage and we walk into the house. My dad goes in first and as he does, he drags his hand along the wall, stepping lightly. He pauses in the hallway. My mom's laugh rings out and my dad rounds the corner like he didn't just try to stealthily sneak into the house. Miss Kim and my mom are chatting over coffee. My mom smiles at my dad and then at me.

"Hi, Miss Kim," I say.

She stands up and gives me a big hug. I hug her back. She seems a little less upset than she'd been the other day but her eyes still look like she's been crying.

"Kim stopped by to say hello," Mom says.

"To invite Boog to dinner," Miss Kim says quickly. She looks at me. "Your mom tells me you're on punishment and so I don't know if you'll be able to come but, well, I miss having someone at the house. It's just me there right now."

My chest tightens up. It makes me sad to think about. I wish Aaron would tell her what's going on.

"Boog is grounded for the foreseeable future," Mom says.

Embarrassment washes over me and I look down at the floor. "I'm sorry, Miss Kim. I messed up so I'm trying to take responsibility for my actions."

Miss Kim raises an eyebrow and for a moment, the corner of her cheek lifts . . . a smile. A genuine smile. "You're such a good kid. Aaron's a good kid, too."

I look her in the eye and she holds my gaze for just a split second longer than she needs to. Something's up.

"I miss him," Miss Kim says. "The not knowing is the worst part but . . ." She touches her lips and lets her gaze wander to the window.

Mom sighs and covers Miss Kim's hand with her own. "One dinner can't hurt," Mom says. She throws me a pointed glance. "We have somewhere to be at six so it'll have to be an early dinner. Can you have her home by five thirty?"

"That works," says Miss Kim, turning back to me. "Want to come with me now? You can help me cook."

I glance at my mom, who gives me a tight smile.

"Sure," I say.

I set down my bag and follow Miss Kim out to her car. The windows are rolled down and as we drive to the end of the block, we pass Melody Olsen. She lives a few houses down from us and she's, like, eight but her parents let her run the streets with her bad little friends. They're walking along giggling and singing a song I recognize but haven't heard in a long time.

"Cross patch, lift the latch, sit by the fire and spin. Take a cup, and drink it up, then call your neighbors in." Melody laughs and then starts the rhyme all over again.

I stick my head out the window and yell at them. "Go home, Melody!"

Melody stops in her tracks and her friends all turn to look at me as we roll by.

"You're not my mama, Booger!" Melody shouts back.

Her friends mean mug me. I can't stand them but I realize they'll probably be safe because they have, like, fifty silver teeth between them. A vamp probably doesn't stand a chance against a pack of musty silver-toothed kids singing vampire rhymes.

They continue their song and I hum along as we drive by. Some of the vampire rhymes are about vampires, like the one in my school folder. But some—like the one Melody is singing with her friends—have been around so long no one knows what they're even supposed to mean.

As we pull into Miss Kim's driveway, Melody continues

down the street and I wonder why she started saying that old rhyme again.

I climb out of the car and notice a large pile of dirt pushed up on the side of Aaron's house.

"Landscaping," Miss Kim says, following my gaze.

"My mom can help. She's digging up our yard right now."

"I'll have to talk to her about it," Miss Kim says. "Come on in."

Everything inside looks pretty much the same as it did the last time I was here. Flyers with Aaron's face litter the dining table, the map of San Antonio with the search grid crisscrossing it.

"Miss Kim, do you want me to wash up so I can help you cook?" I step toward the sink but she cuts me off.

She narrows her eyes at me "No. No, we're not really going to cook dinner. I need to talk to you about something important."

I hold my breath. I knew it.

"I know you know what happened to Aaron," she says.

I lock eyes with her. I brace myself for her reaction. If she's angry, I'll understand. I've been lying to everybody and all it's gotten me is grounded for life. My heart crashes in my chest as I try to think of a way to explain why I'd kept this very important piece of the puzzle from her.

"And I understand why you didn't say anything." Her tone softens and she puts her hand on my shoulder.

"Miss Kim, I—I don't know what happened to him," I say,

stumbling over my words and trying to figure out what to say next.

She smiles. "That's not really a lie, is it? What has happened to him is very . . . unusual."

"I—"

She holds up her hand. "Aaron told me everything."

CHAPTER 20

Miss Kim motions for me to look out her kitchen window. I approach slowly, unsure of what she wants me to see.

"I cut a hole in the floor of the shed," she says. "Dug out enough dirt so that he can lie down."

I stare out at the shed and a wave of relief washes over me. Aaron is safe and he's asleep out there until the sun sets.

Miss Kim stands next to me and lets out a long, slow breath. "I have to know who did this to him," she says. "What kind of monster does this to a child?"

I shake my head. "We've been trying to figure it out. I got in trouble for spraying some kids at school with garlic water."

Miss Kim smiles. "Really? You did that? For Aaron?"

I turn to look at her. "I don't care what he's become. He's still my friend."

Miss Kim's eyes mist over and she bats at her eyes. "I don't know what's going to happen now. All I know is that I have to help him, and even if I can't, he's still my baby. I could never let anyone harm him."

I'd been so worried about what Aaron was going through, how lonely he must be, how afraid he's gotta feel. Me, Jules, and Ced had been running around trying to find the person—vampire—responsible, but I hadn't really stopped to think about how everyday people would react to him if they found out. A terrible fear washes over me. What if they hunt him down and try to destroy him? He isn't some bloodsucking monster. He's Aaron. Or maybe he's both. I don't know but as long as some part of him is still in there I can't let anyone hurt him either.

"Your mom wants you home at five thirty," Miss Kim says. "Aaron can't come out until a little before seven. Do you think we can convince her to let you stay longer?"

I think for a minute. "Maybe."

I boil a pot of water on the stove as Miss Kim cuts up lettuce and tomatoes and pulls a block of cheese over a grater. After we drain the pasta and put on some music, we slap on our best fake smiles and FaceTime my mom.

"Hey," she answers, holding the phone way too close to her face.

"Hey, Mom, just checking in," I say. I point the camera at the food, then at Miss Kim, who crowds in, laughing.

"Hey, Samantha. I just cannot tell you how much I needed this. Boog has made my entire day."

I stare into the phone. "We made pasta and garlic bread and salad and I'm showing Miss Kim how to use Twitter."

"I'm so bad at social media," Miss Kim says.

"Oh, okay," Mom says flatly.

"Can I keep her a little longer?" Miss Kim asks.

My mom's face immediately changes. Her mouth presses into a tight line. "How much longer?"

"Oh, I don't know," says Miss Kim. "Say seven thirty? I can walk her back."

My mom lowers the phone and she says something to my dad, then pops back up. "I'll come get her at seven thirty. I have to run to the store anyway."

That's not true. She never goes to the store this late.

"I appreciate it, Samantha," Miss Kim says.

"Not a problem," my mom says. "Hey, Boog? Can you take me off FaceTime for a minute?" I switch back to the regular phone. Her voice goes from sticky sweet to do-not-play-with-me. "Do not step one toe outside that house till I come to get you. Do you hear me?"

"I promise." I turn to Miss Kim. "Mom said not to let me leave until she gets here."

"Will do," Miss Kim says.

"Seven thirty," says my mom before hanging up.

She's irritated. I can tell, but this is going to be worth it. Aaron did what I asked him to. He went to his mom and she's going to help him. I hope.

Miss Kim doesn't care about the pasta and salad at all. She leans on the kitchen island and takes a deep breath. "I like your mom a lot and I hate lying to her, Boog," she says. "I really do. She and I are the same kind of person and I know she would do anything for you. But I'd do anything for Aaron."

"I told him to come talk to you," I say. "I knew we needed to tell somebody but I didn't know how. We're all really worried that whoever did this to him might come after us, too."

"I understand," Miss Kim says as something dark passes over her face. She comes around the counter and drapes her arm over my shoulder.

I look up into her kind eyes. "I didn't think anyone would believe me. Nobody even believes vampires exist anymore."

"I guess we know better now, don't we?" she asks.

I nod. "I guess we do."

In no time, the sun is setting, casting long shadows through the room. As the sky burns orange outside, there's a tapping at the back door. Miss Kim rushes over and opens it. Aaron comes right in and I assume the invitation was already given. He's covered in a fine layer of dirt. It clings to his hair, his clothing. I look him over, seeing if he's changed in some way I hadn't noticed before but he's still just Aaron. The shy, funny kid who loves Spider-Man and pizza, who had fit in so perfectly with me and Jules and Ced. I can't have that back, can I? I feel like crying.

Miss Kim folds Aaron up in her arms and he hugs her back. When he steps away he catches sight of me and smiles. Miss Kim closes the door and locks it as he walks over to me.

"I'm really glad you talked to your mom," I say.

The relief in Miss Kim's face puts a knot in my throat. Even though I don't think she fully understands what's happening to Aaron—I don't either—having him here is enough for now.

"I'm gonna change my clothes and then we can talk," Aaron says. He gives his mom another hug, then goes upstairs so fast I only catch a glimpse of his ratty T-shirt at the top of the stairs.

I follow Miss Kim into the living room and we sit down across from each other—me in the big overstuffed chair and her on the couch.

"He told me he didn't want to come home because he was afraid of putting me in danger," Miss Kim says.

I glance up the stairs. "He was also afraid that he was gonna scare you," I say. "He didn't want you to be scared of him."

Miss Kim looks thoughtful. She crosses her legs and interlaces her fingers over her knee. "I'm a scientist. I think a lot of people in my field tend to forget that there are things we may never fully understand, that sometimes things aren't quantifiable, or measurable." She sighs. "I was born in a place called Exeter in Rhode Island. Have you ever heard of it?"

Something about that name sounds an alarm bell for me but I can't place it. "Maybe," I say. "I think I heard about it in my Vamp History class."

She nods. "It's a small place with a big history. I'd heard the stories of vampires my whole life. How they'd snatch you away in the night and make a monster of you. I couldn't help but think of those stories when Aaron went missing. Even with what we know happened during the Reaping it never seemed realistic to me that we'd wiped out every single one of them. The Vanquishers retired and everyone acted like that was the end of it, but I always wondered what might happen if we were wrong. Now I know."

"You think the Vanquishers knew it wasn't true?" I can't get my head around that. The Vanquishers are celebrated all around the world for what they did during the Reaping but the doubt creeps in and now I'm starting to question everything. Is that why 'Lita is so hesitant to talk about things or why she insisted me and Jules and Ced wear those little silver chains? Because she had doubts? I quickly pulled the little chain out of my pocket and set on the side table.

"I don't know what the Vanquishers actually knew," Miss Kim says. "I don't think they would have just left us hanging if they knew for a fact that there were any vampires left. Maybe they wanted to believe it or maybe it's something else."

"Like what?" I ask.

Miss Kim lowers her voice. "You're too young to know this but when they retired it was like that." She snaps her fingers. "Almost like somebody told them they didn't have a choice. Like they were forced to go into retirement."

In a rush of cold air Aaron appears on the couch next to his mom. She clutches her chest.

"Aaron, please! You gotta give me a warning or something!"

He's all cleaned up and has on a fresh set of clothes. He smiles. "Sorry."

Miss Kim collects herself and turns to him. "We have to figure out who did this to you if we're going to undo it."

"We've been trying to weed out people at school," I say. "But it's just not working the way we thought it would."

"Aaron is pretty confident that it was someone who was at the skate rink the night he disappeared," Miss Kim says.

"Yeah, but we have to find another way to do the tests because just spraying people with garlic water and trying to see if they show up on camera is not working. I've already been in the counselor's office for it and I can't get in any more trouble. My parents might send me to boot camp or something."

"I'm sorry," Aaron says. "You did all that to help me. This is my fault."

I quickly shake my head. "No. It's not. You didn't ask for this. You didn't do anything wrong and I really want to help you. I just have to think of another way to do it."

"You're a good friend, Boog," Miss Kim says. "I'm glad Aaron has you but you're not alone in this anymore." She closes her hand over Aaron's. "Neither of you is alone."

"So, what do we do now?" I ask.

Miss Kim leans forward, a serious expression stretching across her face. "Let me just walk through this out loud, okay?"

Aaron and I both nod.

"Aaron was bitten and then these changes started to happen. He immediately realized he didn't have a pulse, that he couldn't be out in the sun." She takes a deep breath before continuing. "Then over the next several days other changes occurred." She looks to Aaron to finish.

"I started to crave blood," Aaron says.

"I've got a way to handle that for now," Miss Kim says.

A shiver runs up my back. "Um, do I even wanna know how?"

"I work in a lab with ready access to blood for testing purposes. I may or may not have taken advantage of that." Her gaze drifts to a small blue cooler on the floor next to the couch.

"I was living off squirrels and rats for the first day or two," says Aaron. "I've been knocking back the blood bags my mom brought home like Capri Suns."

I try not to let my face twist up in disgust. I'm not mad at him for doing what he has to do, I just don't want to think about it.

"And I figured out that I'm pretty fast," Aaron continues. "And I can do this." He grips the leg of the big wooden coffee table in front of him and lifts it up over his head like it's weightless. Papers and pencils slide off onto the floor.

"Please put that down before you break it," his mom says.

He sets the table down and I have to physically hold on to the edge of my seat to keep from leaping up and sprinting away. A part of me is absolutely terrified but I stay because there's also a part of me that understands Aaron is still himself under all these new powers. Most of the stuff I know about vampires is about their monstrous abilities. We never talk about how at some point they were regular people who maybe didn't even ask to be vampires themselves.

"Is there anything else you can do?" I ask.

Aaron and his mother exchange glances and she nods.

"Come with me," Aaron says.

He's at the back door before I can stand up. I follow him out into the backyard and Miss Kim sits on the steps. Aaron stands in the center of the yard. I stay a few feet away, unsure of what's about to happen. The sky is dark and clear and the stars are shining. I try to remember if I've ever seen them so bright.

"You okay, Boog?" Aaron asks.

"I should be asking you that," I say.

He looks up at the sky, too. "Everything is different," he says. "It's like I'm seeing everything for the first time. The stars are brighter. The sounds are louder. Everything *feels* different." He levels his eyes at me. "Okay. Ready?"

"Ready for what?" I ask nervously.

Aaron holds out his hand, palm facing up. He closes his eyes. Several seconds go by and nothing changes. I wonder if I'm missing something. Out of the corner of my eye there is movement. I turn to look but whatever it was, it's gone. The hair on the back of my neck stands straight up. Goose bumps rise on my skin.

"Aaron, I—" As I face him, his arm looks like it has turned into a shadow. I can't actually see his hand or forearm at all. In their place is a swirling mass of black mist. I take a step toward him. "What—what is that?"

"I don't know," Aaron says. His face is tight, like he's concentrating really hard. "It's like I can make myself a shadow. It still feels like my arm." He raises it up high and it becomes unnaturally long like a ribbon caught in the wind, stretching out until it almost reaches the house. "I can control it. It's a part of me."

There's a noise somewhere behind me. Miss Kim stands up.

"What was that?" I ask.

Before I can form another thought, something hits me in the back right between my shoulders. The air punches out of my lungs and I fall forward, landing with a thud in the grass. I roll over, gasping for air, my chest burning. Pulling myself up to a sitting position I clutch my back as pain rockets through me. Aaron's arm has returned to its normal appearance and he is in a crouched position, his knees bent, his hands up in front of him, his eyes shining in the dark.

The pain in my back is awful but another feeling is crowding it—fear.

A low growl erupts from Aaron's chest. Standing directly in front of him are two figures.

"You're new," one of them says. He is speaking to Aaron. "You don't understand the rules, but you will."

"I don't know what rules you're talking about," Aaron snaps. His voice is half whisper, half growl.

I stumble to my feet and the other figure steps forward, peering around Aaron and looking me directly in the face. Her hair is a vibrant red color and her eyes are so black they're almost purple. The tips of two razor-sharp teeth poke out from beneath her upper lip as she smiles in a way that makes my blood run cold. Her jaw is too slack, like it's not connected at the hinge. These people are like Aaron.

They are vampires.

"Do you know the rules?" she asks. Now, she's looking right at me. "Your kind should."

"My—my kind?" I ask, confused.

Aaron steps in front of me. "Leave her alone."

Both vampires turn and stare at each other.

"You would protect her?" the woman asks in stunned disbelief. "A Vanquisher?"

Aaron glances at me and I shake my head.

"I'm not a Vanquisher," I say aloud, my voice barely a whisper. I can hardly hear anything over the rush of blood in my ears but I do hear the vampires laughing.

They close in on me and Aaron. Miss Kim takes a bounding step off the porch and is caught in midair as one of the vampires knocks her back. She crumples into a heap on the ground, groaning, clutching her side.

Aaron moves in a flash. He shoves the man back and he flies into the fence. A loud crack splits the night air. I rush to Miss Kim's side and help her to her feet.

Aaron turns to us and his face changes. His jaw comes unhinged, his fangs elongate. I can barely recognize him. I start to scream but nothing comes out. For a moment, I think he's going to attack us but even as his face shifts into something fully inhuman I can still see something familiar in his eyes.

"Run," he says in a voice that sounds like a roar and a scream all at the same time. "Run!"

CHAPTER 21

I pull Miss Kim along the side of the house as a flurry of activity erupts behind us. One of the vampires tries to follow us but he's suddenly knocked into the side of the house, shattering a window and letting out a high-pitched yelp. Miss Kim trips over her own feet.

"No! No! Get up!" I scream. "Please! We have to get out of here!"

Furious growls and bone-splintering crashes echo in the dark. The sound of wood fracturing and more glass shattering fills the night air. I stumble into the street, trying my best to prop up Miss Kim, who winces and groans with each step.

"I think my ribs are broken," she gasps.

"We gotta get to my house!"

I can see it. My house at the end of the cul-de-sac. It

seems too far away as we move toward it. The darkness feels like it's closing in around us and then I realize—it actually is. A swirling mass of black mist is bearing down on us from all sides. The shadows cluster together and make long talons of the swirling dark. The disembodied claws reach for us and fear grips me.

We're not gonna make it to my house.

Suddenly, there's a hand grasping my arm out of the cloud of black shadow. My feet leave the ground and I'm tossed onto the pavement right at the end of my driveway. My stomach turns over as a wave of dizziness crashes over me. My arm aches where it made contact with the pavement and a cut is trickling blood down my forehead. A split second later Miss Kim is on the ground next to me. She staggers to her feet and grabs my arm, pulling me toward my front door.

"Aaron, come on!" I yell.

He materializes out of the black mist and sprints up the drive. Beyond him, halfway down the street the other two vampires are marching toward us. I turn and scramble up my front steps.

"Mom! Dad!" I slam my fists against the door

I hear a shout from inside and the locks click open. Aaron is beside me, holding his mom around the waist. The door swings open. I grab Aaron's hand and try to pull him inside but he bounces off an invisible barrier at the threshold.

"Aaron!" I scream. "You can come in! Get inside!"

Just like that, the barrier is gone and we all fall into the foyer. My dad slams the door shut. He's holding something in his hand. It glints in the light. It's a silver stake as big around as a chair leg.

I scoot back as Aaron disentangles himself from Miss Kim. My mom appears in the doorway to the kitchen. She has something leveled against her shoulder. I recognize what it is almost immediately because I've seen it before. Cedrick has a replica of it. It's the Vanquisher Carmilla's signature weapon. A crossbow. My mom makes a quick movement and in a puff of silvery smoke a stake flies out and strikes Aaron in the shoulder.

He howls so loud my hands instinctively fly to my ears to muffle the sound. Miss Kim crouches over him.

"What did you do?" she wails.

I scramble to Aaron's side. The slender silver stake, launched from the weapon my mom is holding, pokes out of his shoulder. I grab it and yank it out, tossing it aside. A layer of silver dust coats my hand.

"Malika, get back!" my mom shouts. She's taking aim at Aaron again.

Miss Kim drapes her body over him. "Stop! Stop it!"

"Mom!" I yell. "Mom, stop!"

She's not listening. Her eyes are narrowed at Aaron. There is a hardness to her face I've never seen before. She knows exactly what Aaron is and is preparing to destroy him.

I run up to her and stand so that the weapon is pointed directly at me. "Mom! He saved me! But there's more of them out there! Those things would have torn me and Miss Kim apart if he hadn't saved us!"

My mom blinks. She glances at the window. "How many of them are there?"

"I only saw two."

My mom gives a high-pitched whistle and in a flurry of footsteps, Mr. Rupert, followed by Cedrick's dads, Miss Celia, and 'Lita, comes up from the basement.

"Mr. Rupert?" I ask, confused. "Mom, why is he here?"

"Daniel," my mom says, speaking directly to him. "You and Ethan secure the back of the house. The protections should hold but we can't take any chances."

Mr. Rupert, who's apparently on a first-name basis with my mom, follows Mr. Ethan and disappears out the back door. Mr. Alex stays put.

"Celia," 'Lita says from her perch at the front window. "Secure the windows." Miss Celia nods. My mind goes in circles.

Jules emerges from the basement with Cedrick on their heels. Mr. Alex embraces them both. My mom steps toward Aaron as my dad comes up behind her.

"Stop!" I yell. "Tell me what is going on!"

Jules and Cedrick are silent.

"Malika, baby, you don't understand," my mom says.

"No, I don't, but maybe I should!" I stay right in front of Aaron, who has gone mostly silent aside from some whimpering. "I know what Aaron is. He's a vampire but he's not like those ones out there."

My mom's face is unchanged but my dad shakes his head.

"Those other vampires called me a Vanquisher. They said I should know the rules." I glance at my mom's weapon. I watch as my parents and the other adults move around like they've rehearsed this, like they know exactly what they're doing. "Why do you have Carmilla's crossbow?"

Now my mom's expression changes. There is only sadness and fear. She lowers her weapon. "You can't understand how dangerous he will become." She looks at Aaron. "He will crave blood. He will kill to get it. He will kill *you* to get it."

"No he won't," I say. "I've already been around him. He wouldn't hurt me. He's my friend."

My dad puts his hand on my mom's arm. "Samantha, we can't do this. We have to tell her. We have to tell all of them."

"And what about him?" my mom asks, narrowing her eyes at Aaron.

Miss Kim stands up and faces my mom, still clutching her ribs. She's right. She and my mom are a lot alike. They'll both do anything to protect their kids but right now they're on opposite sides.

"This is my son," Miss Kim says defiantly. "I don't know who you people are or why you know so much about this but I won't let you hurt him."

She and my mom stare at each other in tense silence for several moments. I kneel down and cradle Aaron's head in my lap. "Mom. You gotta help him."

Mr. Rupert comes back in with Mr. Ethan.

"It's clear out there," Mr. Ethan says.

"But not in here," Mr. Rupert asks, looking at Aaron. "How are we getting rid of him?"

Miss Kim looks at Mr. Rupert like she's ready to take his head off.

My mom shakes her head. "We're not. Boog, help get him up and put him on the table so we can heal the wound. He was bitten. When? That night at the skate rink?" She thinks for a moment. "That's recent enough that the treatments might still work."

"You can't be serious," Mr. Rupert says angrily. "He's a vampire. The undead. He is the thing your entire order is sworn to vanquish!"

"I know!" my mom shouts back. She takes a deep breath. "I know. But this is a child and even the undead have rules. Never turn a child. They're breaking their rules so I'm breaking ours. Back up, Daniel." My mom squares her shoulders and I have no doubt that if Mr. Rupert takes one step toward Aaron, she'll lay him out.

Mr. Rupert storms into the kitchen as my mom slings down her weapon and helps lift Aaron onto the table as everyone watches on. Jules comes up to me and gives me a hug.

"Our parents brought us over here," they say. "'Lita's been on edge all afternoon. Then she was in the yard and she saw—"

"Shh!" 'Lita hisses from her perch at the window. She clutches the curtain and peers outside.

Everyone falls silent. I grip Jules's hand and my mom moves to 'Lita's side. Mom glances out the window, then turns back and locks eyes with my dad. She clenches her jaw, heaves a sigh that looks like she's just made up her mind about something deadly serious.

"There are two of them out there," my mom says. "We have to handle this."

My dad sprints to the bookcase and taps his fist against the side closest to the wall. A narrow cabinet opens and set inside are a row of gleaming silver stakes. Mr. Ethan reaches into a duffel bag I hadn't even noticed sitting by the front door and pulls out a coiled length of rope. Thin strands of silver are braided throughout its entire length.

My mom sets the crossbow against her shoulder and walks to the front door as Miss Celia and 'Lita stand in front of me, Cedrick, and Jules. Aaron lies motionless on the table as my heart crashes in my chest.

"Mom?"

She looks back at me and I expect to see fear, sadness, but to my surprise there is none of that. There is only fierce determination . . . and a smile.

My dad crouches behind her, a silver stake in each hand and another one tucked into the waist of his pants. Mr. Ethan unfurls his rope and sets his left hand on my dad's back. My mom yanks the door open. One of the vampires who had chased us down the street is standing in the front yard. The other one is a little farther down the drive.

Their eyes are black and their mouths hang open. Oozing dark liquid drips from their ragged lips and their fingers taper to points like claws. My mom rushes forward, my dad at her side, Mr. Ethan behind them. I try to run after them but 'Lita grabs me and holds me back.

"Mom!" I scream.

There's a thud at the back of the house and Miss Celia rushes into the kitchen. Jules slides past me and as 'Lita turns to grab them I slip her grip and rush to the open front door. It takes me a minute to fully comprehend what I'm seeing.

Mr. Ethan has his rope around the ankle of the vamp with the red hair as she kicks and screams. The screeching sound coming from her is like nails on a chalkboard. She lashes out, making her arm long and shadowy the same way Aaron had. She swipes at my mom, who ducks out of the way as my dad hurls one of his stakes at the vamp. The redhead easily dodges it but while she's distracted my mom does a barrel roll, sets the bow against her shoulder, and fires a silver stake directly into the vamp's chest.

"What?!" Cedrick screams.

My heart jumps into my chest. I hadn't even realized he'd come up next to me.

The vampire wails in agony and then begins to glow, as if she's burning from the inside out. Her skin turns a fiery orange, like the sky at sunset. My mom steps closer and watches, unmoved, as the vampire turns to a column of ash. Mr. Ethan whips his rope around and it cuts through the vampire-shaped heap of ash and it scatters into the night air.

My mom, my dad, and Mr. Ethan rush back inside and slam the door shut.

"Where's the other one?" my mom asks, her chest heaving.

"Here!" 'Lita calls from somewhere out back.

We all make a beeline straight to the backyard, where the other vamp is laid out in the grass, a long silver sword pinning him to the ground. Smoke billows from his back and the bottoms of his feet. 'Lita leans on the weapon as Miss Celia kneels by the vamp's head.

"Who is doing this?" Miss Celia demands. "Who is in charge of your hive?"

The vamp twists his body around and opens his mouth. He is trying to bite Miss Celia.

"We're not going to get anything out of this one," Miss Celia says.

'Lita shrugs and in one quick motion, yanks the sword out of the vamp's shoulder. He's immediately up and at the rear fence in the blink of an eye. Something whizzes past my face and embeds itself in the left side of the vampire's back. He turns to face us. The tip of a silver stake sticks out of his chest, right where his cold dead heart should be. Me, Jules, and Ced turn to see that my dad is the one who threw it. His hand is still raised in front of him. He smiles.

"Got him," he says.

The vampire collapses to his knees and 'Lita marches up to him as he turns to dust. She raises her leg and kicks him hard in the chest. He disintegrates into a million weightless pieces of ash that float up into the nighttime sky.

'Lita presses a button on the side of the sword and the blade retracts into the handle. She slips it in her pocket and comes to stand in front of us.

"A little help!" Mr. Alex hollers from inside.

Mr. Ethan bounds inside and when we join him, we find both Miss Kim and Mr. Alex pinning Mr. Rupert facedown on the living room floor, one of my dad's glinting stakes in his hand.

CHAPTER 22

I rush up to him and kick the stake away. "What were you doing with that?"

He grunts angrily and Mr. Alex presses his knee into Mr. Rupert's back.

"He tried to stake my son!" Miss Kim wails.

"Mr. Rupert!" Jules screams. "You stupid jerk! Leave Aaron alone!"

Mr. Rupert thrashes around on the ground. "Get off me!"

My mom steps in front of Aaron and glances at Miss Kim. "You saw what I did to the vamp in the front yard?"

Miss Kim nods as worry clouds her face.

"I'll do the same thing to Daniel if he takes a single step toward Aaron."

Miss Kim and my mom have an understanding and

Miss Kim stands up. Mr. Alex does, too, and Mr. Ethan embraces him.

Mr. Rupert is disheveled and his bald head is gleaming with sweat. "He must be destroyed!"

"Listen to me," my mom says in a tone that makes me feel like I'm in trouble, too. "I'm going to tend to his wound and you are going to take your triflin' behind in the kitchen and be quiet."

"I—" Mr. Rupert begins.

'Lita's sword pops open with a soft swishing sound. "Oh no. How did that happen?" Sarcasm drips from each word.

Cedrick leans in close to me. "'Lita is gonna slice him up." He almost sounds happy about it.

The threat, that doesn't sound as much like a threat as a promise, is clear and Mr. Rupert stomps into the kitchen.

We huddle around Aaron, watching my mom tend to his wounded shoulder. She packs it with a fibrous material she'd taken out of her workbag.

"This will draw the silver dust out and allow the injury to heal," she says as she carefully bandages his shoulder.

"What is that stuff?" I ask.

"It's a synthetic wound-healing mesh. Normally, a vampire could heal this kind of injury on their own but my weapon is tipped with silver dust. If it had stayed in his shoulder any longer . . ." She trails off. "Doesn't matter. You got it out in time and this will help him heal."

"Where'd you get it?"

"The mesh? It's my design. From back in the day."

Miss Kim stays by Aaron's side, caressing his face as his eyes open and close. He looks like himself except for the little pointy teeth.

"He'll be sick for a few days, but he'll be okay," my mom says. "I'm sorry." She bites her bottom lip as she fights back tears.

"I'd say it's okay but it's not," Miss Kim says.

"I know," says Mom. "But this is what I've been trained to do."

Miss Kim doesn't respond. I don't blame her for being angry at my mom. I'm angry, too. This is what they've been keeping from me and it's not some small thing. As Aaron drifts into unconsciousness, my mom steers me to the kitchen where everyone, aside from Aaron and his mom, is gathered.

"I don't know where to start," my mom says. "So I'll just lay it all out. We are all that is left of the Vanquishers."

"I know where we should start," Mr. Rupert huffs. "How about with your betrayal of your oath."

"How about we start with the way your hairline betrayed you?" Mr. Alex says angrily. "Let's start there."

Cedrick claps his hand over his mouth to stifle a laugh as his dads stare down Mr. Rupert.

"Wait," I say. "So obviously Mr. Rupert's not a vampire."

Mr. Rupert looks at me like he's never been more disgusted in his entire life. "How dare you even suggest—"

"I'm gonna need you to keep your attitude in check," my dad says. "Boog has questions and she's not wrong for asking."

I glare at Mr. Rupert. "And he's not a Vanquisher?"

"No," says my mom firmly. "He's not. And he should remember that."

"I am the sanctioned record keeper of the Vanquishers and—"

"Enough," my dad says. "Look. We owe the kids an explanation and we need to figure out what we're going to do now that it's clear a new hive has been established."

"A new hive?" Jules asks. "Is that really what's happening? But you guys killed the two vamps outside."

"There are more," 'Lita says. "I'm certain of it."

Miss Celia pulls Jules close.

My mom takes a deep breath and leans on the counter. "Me, your dad, Ethan, Celia, and of course 'Lita were—are— Vanquishers. Mr. Rupert is our official record keeper. And Alex knows about us but has been an unwavering ally. We are all that's left after the Reaping. We were forced to retire but we have kept our ears to the ground in case things got bad again. We have a strict policy of destroying the undead on sight. No exceptions but—" She glances to the dining room where Aaron is laid out on the table.

"Things have changed," 'Lita says.

Everyone turns to her.

"We cannot pick up where we left off," 'Lita continues. "We have to find a way forward that includes helping Aaron."

"I might have a way to do that." Miss Kim is standing in the kitchen doorway. "If I can take some time to analyze his blood, to look at exactly what's happening inside, I might be able to find a way to reverse this."

"Samples have been tightly controlled," my mom says. "Access to them is regulated."

"By who?" Miss Kim asks.

My mom's brow furrows. "Most of them are in the possession of various government agencies. But look, if you're going to try and reverse it, I hate to say it but we've tried."

"It can't be done," Mr. Rupert says. He turns to Miss Kim. "Your son is a monster."

Miss Kim steps forward and is about to cuss him out but I beat her to it.

"He's not a monster," I say. "But you might be. You're so angry. You're rude and I don't like the way you're always following me and my friends around. You need to get a hobby or something."

"My hobby is keeping you and your friends alive," Mr. Rupert says through an angry pout. "And my surveillance of you is only going to get worse because now that you understand your connection to the Vanquishers, you'll need to start your own training and guess who will be in charge of that?"

"What training?" I ask, turning to my mom.

"Pipe down, Daniel," my dad says.

"Vanquishers are not chosen at random," Miss Celia says. "Usually we pass down this responsibility from generation to generation."

"You were supposed to start your training a year ago," says Mr. Rupert, eyeing our parents.

I turn to 'Lita.

"To become Vanquishers yourselves one day," she says.

My mom moves closer to me. "After the Reaping, after we retired, we had a choice to make. We could bring you into the fold the way it's been done for generations or we could try to do something else. We could try to leave the past behind us. We wanted to believe the world didn't really need us anymore and that maybe we could spare you the responsibility of having to shoulder this burden. But we don't have that choice anymore."

I step away from her. "No. I don't wanna have anything to do with the Vanquishers if it means I have to hurt Aaron. I won't do it."

"You don't have a choice," Mr. Rupert huffs.

"Yes, she does," my dad says. "You have a choice, Boog. You can learn about our history, about the parts of vampire lore that they don't teach you in school. You can learn how to fight. But maybe now with everything that's happened to Aaron you can also learn the best ways to help him avoid becoming the monster. Being a Vanquisher can mean something else for you, maybe for all of us."

"I just need some time to figure out how to save him," Miss Kim says, her voice pleading.

"I can get you access to a lab, to samples, equipment," my mom says. "Whatever you need."

"I cannot believe you're seriously considering this," Mr. Rupert says.

"Believe it," I snap. "The only way I'm doing this, the only way I'm letting you tell me what to do is if you promise right here and now that you won't do anything to hurt Aaron."

Mr. Rupert laughs but 'Lita clears her throat. "Swear it, Daniel," she says. "Now."

The color drains from his face. 'Lita's got this man shaking in his boots and I'm living for it.

"I swear," Mr. Rupert says before turning his back and storming off like a kid who just got in trouble.

"Our manifesto has always been to vanquish the undead," my mom says as everyone crowds around the island in the kitchen. Jules loops their arm through mine and Cedrick gives me a knowing little smile. "We're still going to do that, of course, because as you'll soon find out, most vampires are not like Aaron. Most of them are mindless monsters."

"I'm gonna slice up so many vamps," Cedrick says. "Not Aaron. Not him. But the bad ones? Yeah. Slice them right up." His dad nudges him and he goes quiet.

My mom eyes him and then continues. "You will train to protect yourselves against the undead, learn the histories, and maybe one day learn to fight on the offensive but not right now. Right now, our goal is to find out who attacked Aaron and why. It's not random that it happens to be your close friend who was bitten, the first recorded attack in twenty years and it's the friend of a Vanquisher's kid?"

"It can't be coincidence," Mr. Alex says.

"I'm positive it's not," says my mom. "And that means that we might already be targets. We have to consider that someone knows who we are and where we are."

"They obviously know where 'Lita is, right?" Mr. Alex asks. "Her cover's been blown for years but what are the odds they knew about the rest of you?"

The room goes dead quiet. The thought of some hidden hive of vamps keeping tabs on us makes my stomach queasy. I think about all the ways my parents have been trying to keep me safe and how I'd just brushed it off. "Guilt" isn't a strong enough word.

"I'm really sorry I put us in danger," I say. "I never meant to. I just wanted to help Aaron."

My mom cups my face in her hands and looks me right in the eyes. "What happened to Aaron is not your fault and if I had been more open with you, you might've understood why we did the things we did." She sighs and presses her forehead against mine. "There's still so much to explain but I think we'll save that for another time. I promise you, we'll do what we can to help Aaron and to make sure that these vamps don't become more of a problem."

I hug my mom tight and as I do a little burst of air rushes past me. Aaron is suddenly standing in the kitchen. My dad tenses up. Miss Celia moves her hand to her waist and I wonder what weapon might have hung there at some point. I let go of my mom and go to Aaron, putting my arms around him and hugging him tight. There are suddenly more arms around us as Jules and Cedrick join the group hug.

"We're in this together," I say to Aaron.

"Like superheroes without the tight costumes," Cedrick says. "Speaking of heroes . . ." He turns back to our parents. "We knew 'Lita was the Mask of Red Death but, Dad, you're Sailor's Knot?"

Mr. Ethan nods and then tilts his head to the side. "You know how hard it's been to keep that from you when all you ever talk about is Carmilla?"

"I mean, did you see the way she ended that vamp?" He beams at my mom.

Mr. Ethan just laughs.

"Daddy is Threshold," Mom says.

My dad winks at my mom. "I told you Carmilla was my favorite," he says.

"I'm Argentium," Miss Celia says.

"I told you about Nightside," 'Lita says. "She and Dayside were lost during the Reaping. We disbanded the Wrecking Crew months before, when things got dark. We're all that's left."

A hush falls over the room. It feels like a weight has been lifted. Now that it's all out in the open, I breathe a little easier.

"We're moving into uncharted territory," says 'Lita. "Best to be prepared for anything. You should begin your training right away."

As I keep my arms around Aaron, as my parents watch me and Cedrick and Jules embrace our friend, it feels like we're bridging a gap between people on two sides of a huge gulf— vampires on one side and vampire hunters on the other. Until today, I didn't even know this battle was still raging but since it is, and since my friend Aaron is here with me, maybe it means things can change.

ONE WEEK LATER

The basement used to be my dad's man cave. Then I took over and it was the homework-movie-sleepover cave. Now the TV is pushed to the side, the couch is gone, and there's a big table set up in the center. The windows are blacked out with paint and my mom hung up a bunch of big dry-erase boards on the back wall. As me and Cedrick and Jules sit waiting for Mr. Rupert to come in and start his first lesson in our Vanquisher training program, that he's spent way too much time crafting, I take out my phone and text Aaron.

ME: Text me when you get up.

Cedrick leans back and looks up at the ceiling. "Boog, where did your dad get these chairs? My butt cheeks are asleep. There's not even no cushion or nothing."

"Garage sale," I say. "You know he can't pass up a deal."

Jules wiggles around in their chair. "Mine sounds like it's going to break."

"Switch it out with Mr. Rupert's," I say.

Jules switches out the seat and sits down right as Mr. Rupert comes stomping down the stairs. We sit around acting like we aren't up to anything, which makes him immediately suspicious. I try not to look at him.

"Something I need to be aware of?" he asks as he sets down a stack of books.

"Probably," Cedrick says under his breath.

Mr. Rupert bends to sit in his chair. I hold my breath but he suddenly stands straight up and leans on the table.

"I know you don't take this seriously," he says.

"We've never done this before," Jules says. "It's literally day one."

"This isn't Mrs. Lambert's class. You don't get to just do what you please. I have rules and you will—"

"Daniel!" my dad calls from upstairs where him and my mom are having coffee. "I need you to bring it down a notch before you blow out the vein in your forehead."

Mr. Rupert readjusts his jacket and takes a deep breath. "Lesson one will comprise vampire lore and Vanquisher origins. Take out something to write with and please, pay attention because I don't like repeating myself."

We do as we're asked and it makes me way too happy to know that Mr. Rupert is gonna have to rein in his old-man rage. He pulls up his chair and sits down. There's a loud crack and one of the chair legs shoots off and bounces across the floor as Mr. Rupert lands flat on his back.

Day one of Vanquisher training academy is already a success.

ACKNOWLEDGMENTS

Writing a vampire story has been on my author bucket list forever. I've been fascinated by vampire stories for as long as I can remember. I have read everything Anne Rice ever wrote. I own no less than seven copies of Bram Stoker's *Dracula*. I'm obsessed with the Marvel comic version of *Dracula*. I am a student of Octavia Butler's *Fledgling*. I'm incredibly excited that my initial contribution to the world of vampire literature is a middle grade title because young readers deserve these kinds of vampire tales, too.

The Vanquishers takes place in the city of San Antonio because the city left an impression on me. I moved to San Antonio in 2017 and found a vibrant community, some of the best food I've ever had, and a network of writers and bookish folks who helped me find my way into publishing. I was in San

Antonio when I learned that my debut novel, *Cinderella Is Dead*, would be published. I launched that book and my second novel, *This Poison Heart*, into the world from my home right outside of San Antonio. I wrote most of *The Vanquishers* right there in that house, and it is for these reasons that San Antonio holds a special place in my heart. Thank you to the city of San Antonio for inspiring this story.

As I write these acknowledgments, my work is being challenged in the state of Texas, with some school districts pulling my work from shelves. Young readers are being denied access to books about people from historically marginalized and excluded backgrounds. The entire ordeal is incredibly disheartening but it will not dissuade me from continuing to write stories that center *us*. What I want to say to my readers is that I see you, and I know there is a place for you in the pages of the vast and varied landscape of children's literature. Storytelling is such a powerful tool for understanding. It can allow us to cultivate empathy for one another, it can challenge the way we see the world, and we can learn to be better people because of it. I'm truly honored to be able to do this work.

I'd like to say a special thank-you to all the educators and librarians who have stood firm during these challenging times and who have always put the needs of their students first. Thank you for continuing to put my work in the hands of the readers who need it most. I'm so grateful for your support.

I'd like to take a moment to thank my agent, Jamie Vankirk;

my editor, Mary Kate Castellani; my publicist, Alexa Higbee; and the entire team at Bloomsbury. Getting these stories out into the world is a team effort and I'm incredibly lucky to be able to be a part of this amazing network of people.

Thank you to my family—Mike, Amya, Ny, Elijah, and Lyla. I love you all so much. Thank you to my brother, Spencer, love you so much. Thank you to my auntie Rolanda, who watched me write my very first novel when I was nineteen and encouraged me to keep going. Rest in power. See you when I get there.

I'd like to extend my sincerest thanks to the team at Buffalo Street Books here in Ithaca, New York. Big shout-out to Lisa, Isis, Isabella, and the entire team for making me feel so welcome and for championing my work. Thank you, BSB fam!

And to my readers, THANK YOU! I'm so appreciative of each and every one of you. Thank you for supporting my work and for your boundless enthusiasm. You all are the reason I write. Thank you and happy reading.